THE KILLINGS

AN OLIVIA MILLER MYSTERY THRILLER
BOOK 1

J. A. WHITING

To hear about new books and book sales, please sign up for my mailing list at:

www.jawhitingbooks.com

❀ Created with Vellum

For my twisted sister, with love

December 15, 1943 - January 6, 2015

A huge yellow-orange moon rose over the treetops as wisps of dark clouds passed over its glowing face. Olivia Miller and her roommate, Melissa, walked along the brick sidewalk of the Somerville, Massachusetts neighborhood near the edge of the university campus.

"Look at the moon." Melissa's brown eyes beamed as she gestured to the sky with the bottle of red wine she was holding.

"It looks just like a Halloween moon." Olivia carried a plate of freshly-baked chocolate chip cookies. "Perfect for tonight."

Olivia and Melissa were dressed as crows. The young women and two of their friends had spent hours cutting and sewing to create matching costumes of black pants and black sweatshirts covered in fabric feathers with yellow beaks attached to the hoods. Pleased with how the costumes had come out, they were proud of their idea to be a "murder of crows" for the night's pre-Halloween party.

Strolling along the tree-lined streets, the two friends passed two and three-decker apartment houses. Some of the houses were owned by families or long-time Somerville residents and others were rented by university students. The groups peacefully co-existed in this area of the city, unlike in other parts where students were often rowdy and noisy which resulted in the residents calling the police to complain.

Many of the homes had pots of colorful mums sitting side by side with carved pumpkins decorating the front porches. At the end of the month, children would take to the sidewalks disguised as ghosts and witches and vampires on the prowl for candy to fill their bags.

"I really shouldn't be going out tonight." The light breeze caught Olivia's long, brown hair and swirled some strands into her face. "I have to get my applications finished and I have a paper due on Monday."

"Those law school applications can wait," Melissa said. "I need to get my med school apps finished, but it's important to have some fun ... and you've been working on that paper all week. We don't have to stay at the party long. A couple of hours and then we can head home if we want. We shouldn't be hermits. It's our senior year of college. We should be able to have some fun and not just study and work all the time."

Olivia knew that Melissa was right. Both of them had been buried in school work and Olivia was looking forward to relaxing, listening to music, and talking with friends.

"I'm glad Colleen invited us to the party," Olivia said. "I know she lives with a couple of guys. I've seen them around, but I've never met them."

"I hung out with Gary once or twice with a bunch of other friends," Melissa said. "I don't know him well at all, but he seemed fun. I've never met Christian though."

The girls approached the apartment building where the party was to be held. It was a brick structure of six levels with four apartments on each floor.

Several people dressed in costumes heading out to other parties passed the young women on the side street. The breeze kicked up again and rustled the leaves around their feet as a cloud hid the moon and blocked its light.

"Are we early?" Olivia looked up at the second floor windows. There were a few lights on in Colleen's apartment, but she couldn't hear voices or music playing and didn't see anyone moving around inside.

"We must be," Melissa groaned. "I hate being first."

Walking up the front porch steps to the landing,

Melissa scanned the mailbox names looking for the button to press for the correct apartment.

"The door's open," Olivia said. "No need to buzz."

Stepping into the small lobby, they climbed the staircase to the second floor apartment.

"Mel, do we even have the right night?" Olivia asked uneasily. "It's so quiet. I can't hear anyone inside." She knocked on the apartment door and the pressure from her hand nudged it open a crack. A prickle of anxiety ran through Olivia's body.

Melissa put her hand on the door and pushed it wider. "Hey? Anyone home?" She stepped into the small entryway.

Several shoes were lined up on a mat along the right side of the entry. Jackets hung from white hooks screwed into the wall above the shoes.

Olivia hesitated. She didn't understand why, but something felt off. Under her jacket, a flash of panic skittered over her skin and she had the urge to run away. Trying to brush off the sensation, she followed Melissa into the apartment.

Three bikes leaned against the left side wall of the entryway.

"Colleen?" Melissa called. "Where is everybody?"

Walking from the entry through the dead-silent main hallway, Melissa stopped short at the living room's arched entrance and Olivia almost collided into her back.

"Liv." Melissa's voice squeaked in her throat. "No, no." The bottle of wine slipped from her hand, clunked against the wood floor, and rolled a few inches away.

"What is it?" When Olivia looked over Melissa's shoulder, her throat constricted and she gagged. Her hands trembled so violently that she almost dropped the plate of cookies.

Melissa spun around, pushed past Olivia, and ran out of the apartment back into the second floor hall. Standing near the staircase, hunched over, breathing hard, she made a pitiful wailing sound.

Olivia took a shaky step into the living room, her eyes wide with shock.

A young man was face up on the floor in front of the couch. It was Gary.

Blood soaked through the front of the skeleton costume. His wide eyes stared unseeing at the ceiling.

Olivia shifted her gaze to the right side of the room.

Sprawled in an easy chair, Christian's upper body hung over the arm of the seat at a weird angle. A cowboy hat had fallen from his head. Blood dripped from a gash in his throat and formed a puddle on the floor next to the chair. His arms hung loose. He was wearing a fringed suede vest over what was once a white T-shirt ... now it was red. Christian's skin was ghostly pale.

A strange metallic smell filled Olivia's nostrils. As

she stared at the blood puddle, another drop fell from Christian's throat.

Her stomach clenched and blood roared in her ears. Olivia wanted to run, but her limbs were so weak that she couldn't summon the enormous effort required to move them. All she could do was stand frozen and helpless in the doorway.

The room started to spin and Olivia placed one hand against the wall. Her eyes moved over the bodies, the blood. Her brain, sluggish and slow, struggled to process what was before her. She had never seen a young person dead.

The image was so unnatural that part of her brain expected the young men to sit up and laugh, the whole scene staged by them as an early Halloween stunt to frighten the guests arriving for the party.

Olivia glanced down at the plate in her hand and was struck by how stupid and trivial it was to still be holding a platter of cookies.

Melissa whimpered in the hall.

Olivia forced her feet to move and she took several slow, backward steps out of the living room. Her senses so heightened, everything seemed to be shimmering and buzzing.

Voices and footsteps could be heard on the stairwell.

Olivia sucked in a breath trying to clear her head and she turned around to face the open front door of the apartment. Her legs moved as if she was wading through quicksand.

The group of people arriving saw Melissa at the top of the landing and called to her.

Melissa cried out.

Olivia heard footsteps rushing up the stairs.

A young woman wearing a witch's hat wrapped her arm around Melissa's shoulders and leaned close to determine what was wrong.

Olivia didn't recognize the tall, young man who stepped into the apartment. A dark-haired woman dressed as a mouse followed behind him.

The man took one look at Olivia standing at the living room entrance and rushed forward. "Oh, hell," he muttered when he saw Gary and Christian in the living room. He knew they were dead. No one could lose all that blood and live, but he hurried to the bodies anyway to check for pulses.

Olivia and the young woman wearing the mouse costume had been in some classes together ...Ynes Clinton took tentative steps forward, glanced quickly at the carnage in the living room, turned her head away and grasped Olivia's arm.

Olivia blinked at Ynes. "Do you have a phone?" Her throat was so constricted that her voice came out tinny and hoarse.

Ynes nodded.

Olivia managed to ask, "Can you call 911?" She had

a phone in her own pocket, but her brain was so befuddled that she wasn't thinking right. She straightened as a thought flashed through her mind. Adrenaline flooded Olivia's body. She shoved the cookie plate into Ynes' hands and whirled.

"Colleen!" Olivia called out as she rushed down the hall, glancing first into the kitchen and then into the bathroom.

"Olivia, no," Ynes shouted. "The killer could be hiding in the apartment."

Ignoring Ynes' warning, Olivia pushed open the bedroom door on her right and looked in. "Colleen?" The room was empty.

When she turned back into the hallway, a figure stepped through the far bedroom's door, the last room on the left of the corridor.

Olivia stopped short, her heart jumped into her throat.

The figure, dressed in black with a black ski mask over his face, hesitated for a half- second, making eye contact with Olivia.

"Someone's here," Olivia screamed over her shoulder.

The figure wheeled and fled through the open door into the back hall of the apartment building to the rear staircase.

Olivia held back for a second, but then started after the person to see if she could get another look at him from the second level porch when he ran out the door of the building's first floor.

As she passed the next bedroom, something caught her eye and she halted at the entrance to the room. A tube of mascara and its brush wand lay on the floor in front of a desk. Olivia stared at the tube and the tiny brush and gingerly entered the room.

"Colleen?" she whispered, afraid of what she would find. With her heart pounding, Olivia's eyes darted around the small space. Shaking like a leaf in hurricane, she forced herself to kneel and check under the bed. Nothing.

A muffled sound came from the closet. Olivia turned to the noise, holding her breath. She stood, faced the door, and crossed the room by moving her feet a few inches at a time. Reaching for the doorknob, she pulled her hand back for a moment, then sucked in a breath, grabbed the knob, and flung the closet door wide.

A long breath escaped from her lungs.

Colleen, curled in a ball, lay trembling on the closet floor.

Olivia knelt and gently put her hands on Colleen's arms. "Are you hurt?"

Colleen shook her head. Whimpering, she wrapped her arms around Olivia's waist and buried her face into her shoulder. Olivia hugged the young woman and rocked her, rubbing her back.

"Can you stand?" Olivia helped Colleen to her feet. "You're okay. You're safe," she murmured to the shaking girl.

Ynes peered into the room and exhaled. "Thank heavens," she whispered when she saw Olivia and Colleen standing together just inside the closet.

Olivia helped Colleen to the bed and the two of them sat. Tears poured from Colleen's eyes, she wheezed and ran her hands through her hair. Her whole body shook.

"I heard it. What did they do?" Colleen gasped.

Olivia and Ynes exchanged a glance.

Colleen saw what passed between them and started to wail. "No!" Her eyes danced wildly around the room and she shifted her body closer to Olivia. Her chest heaved. "Where's Christian? Where's Gary?" she whispered.

Olivia took Colleen's hands in hers. She didn't know what to say to the trembling young woman.

"The police," Ynes said. "I hear the siren. They're almost here."

2

A bout ten young people had entered the apartment between the time Olivia and Melissa arrived and when the police answered the emergency call. The cops were not pleased that the crime scene had been compromised by so many people going in and out of the place before they showed up. One officer ushered the young men and women out of the apartment and down to the sidewalk where he and another officer took statements and sorted out who arrived when to the apartment. A woman officer came in and took over the duty of speaking with Colleen.

Everyone milled around outside while detectives and police officers interviewed people one at a time. A tall, red haired college student with freckles scattered over his cheeks stepped away from a group of young people who had been in the apartment and approached Melissa and Olivia. The girls recognized him from campus. He introduced himself as Jack Wilson and said he was a senior at the university.

"You found the bodies?" he asked.

Olivia and Melissa nodded.

"I went into the apartment just before the cops arrived. I was hanging around out back for a while. I can't believe this happened," Jack said.

Jack's words caused something to ping in Olivia's brain. "Which way did you come in? Front or back stairs?"

"I came up the back staircase."

Taking a step closer, Olivia asked, "Did you happen to see a guy dressed in black wearing a ski mask leave out the back way?"

Jack's eyes widened. "Yeah. Actually, two people left the building wearing ski masks. Why?"

"You saw him?" Olivia's voice was excited. "Wait. *Two* people wearing ski masks left the building?"

"One passed me on the stairs. Why? Who is he?"

Olivia said, "He was in the apartment hiding in one of the bedrooms. What happened when he passed you?"

"Is he the killer?" Jack asked.

"I don't know. Maybe."

"The killer passed me?" Shock made the young man's muscles tense and Jack's speaking rate sped up.

"One person in a ski mask came out while I was smoking outside the back entrance ... before I went up to Gary and Christian's. The second guy in a mask ran down the stairs when I was on the way up. I didn't think anything of it. A few people left the building in costumes while I was outside. A couple of witches, a clown, a zombie. I figured they were just coming and going to Halloween parties." He shook his head. "The killer wore a ski mask? I could have tackled him ... if, I only knew."

Olivia's mind raced. *Were two people working together? Were there two killers?*

"Two people were wearing ski masks?" Melissa said. The muscles around her mouth quivered and she looked as if she might cry. "Two killers?"

"They didn't seem like they were together," Jack offered. "They left separately."

"Did you get a look at them? Were any parts of their faces visible? Did you notice anything about them that stood out?" Olivia asked.

"Nothing, no. I don't know. I didn't really pay attention." Jack's facial expression changed to fear. "The first one, though, he looked me in the eye. Something about the look he gave me made me feel weird." Jack ran his hand over the top of his head. "The killer went right by me? I can't believe it."

"Did you see a knife?" Olivia asked. "Was either guy carrying a knife?"

Jack thought for a second. "I didn't notice a knife."

A detective walked up to the girls and interrupted their conversation with Jack. He moved Melissa and Olivia closer to one of the squad cars. After the young women talked with the detective, they were led to the back seat of the police car and taken to headquarters where they were questioned further.

Pictures of the scene flashed through Olivia's mind and she wondered if the images would burn into her brain forever from having to tell and retell what she found in that apartment.

The lights in the police station reflected off the stark white walls and the brightness made Olivia wish she had a pair of sunglasses. Every cell in her body seemed to emit a low-level hum like her system was on high alert. Colors and sounds cut into her eyes and ears. Scents were too sharp. Her skin was tingling like when she had a fever.

It was one o'clock in the morning when they finished at the police station and a cab picked the women up and returned them, still wearing their crow costumes, to their own apartment building in Somerville. Melissa and Olivia dragged themselves up the stairs to their sixth-floor apartment and went to the tiny kitchen where Melissa collapsed at the small table and put her head facedown on top of her arms. Her long black hair spread over the wooden surface.

"I'm going to make tea," Olivia told her.

"I'm too exhausted to even swallow," Melissa mumbled.

Olivia put the water on, took out two mugs, tea bags, and some milk. She sat across from Melissa to wait for the water to boil. Her shoulders hunched forward, her muscles suffering the after-effects of the adrenaline that had rushed through her body earlier in the night.

"What the heck happened back there, Mel?" Olivia asked. Her nerves on edge, she fiddled with the empty cup on the table.

Melissa raised her head and looked at Olivia with teary, red-rimmed eyes. "Who would kill them? Why?"

"Drugs?"

Melissa shook her head. "Colleen didn't do drugs."

"But, did the guys? Did they sell drugs?" Olivia asked.

"Absolutely not. Colleen wouldn't have anything to do with drugs. She wouldn't live with people who did drugs. The guys were athletes."

"Athletes can do drugs."

"Not these guys," Melissa said. "Colleen knew Gary and Christian from her home town. They've been friends for years, since they were little kids. They went to school together. That's how they were sharing an apartment here. The guys graduated last May. Christian was working at a start-up in Cambridge. Gary was working as a math teacher at a middle school in Boston."

"The killer was there when we got to the apartment." Olivia crossed her arms over her chest and hugged herself. "If we were a few minutes earlier..."

She and Melissa exchanged frightened looks.

"Did we just miss getting killed?" Melissa's voice shook. Her face was pale. "Did you get a good look at that person in the hallway?"

Olivia's facial muscles tensed. "Not really. It was dark in the hall. He might have been a bit taller than me, but it was hard to tell. Slender. He was dressed all in black, had the ski mask on." She hesitated. "He looked me in the eye. I didn't see his face, but he sure got a good look at *me*."

"Oh, no," Melissa breathed. "Do you think...?" She paused and her forehead wrinkled with concern.

"He'll come looking for me?" A shudder shook Olivia's body. "I don't know." She rubbed her forehead. "Why would he? He knows I couldn't make out his face. It would be too risky to come after me." She tried to convince herself as much as Melissa. "Wouldn't the best thing be for the killer to just lay low? Let things blow over."

The tea kettle produced a loud shriek and both women jumped. Olivia dragged herself to the stove, lifted the kettle, and poured the boiling water into the mugs. She carried the tea to the table and sank down onto the chair.

Melissa put her hands around her mug. "What about what Jack saw? Do you think there were two killers? Those two people in ski masks ... were they together?"

"It's possible," Olivia said. "It's also possible they weren't."

"Do you think the killer knew there was going to be a party?" Melissa asked.

"Seems sort of dumb to plan to kill two guys right before a bunch of people are going to show up for a party," Olivia said. "But, anything's possible."

"The killer must have known the guys," Melissa said. "It couldn't have been random. Could it?"

"I guess it could've been. The front door was open. It was easy to get in." Olivia was thinking out loud. "The guys were sitting in the living room. Maybe they knew him because they were sitting, like they were just relaxing. But, if the killer came in wearing a ski mask, they would have thought he was there for the party."

"Yeah, they probably thought the ski mask was a costume. So either they knew the killer or they didn't suspect anything because they were just thinking it was someone who came for the party," Melissa said.

"Either way, the killer would have had to act fast. He could have taken the first guy by surprise, but the second one would have tried to defend himself," Olivia said. "He wouldn't just sit there waiting for the killer to come over to him. That must be why Gary was on the floor in front of the couch. Christian was probably stabbed first, and then Gary stood up to fight the attacker. The killer had to attack before the guys could really react. Or maybe there were two killers and each one took out one of the guys?"

The friends sat in silence for a few minutes thinking over different scenarios.

Olivia said, "Was the killer after only one of them or did he intend to kill both of them? What was the reason?"

"What about Colleen?" Melissa asked. "Was she supposed to be a victim, too?"

"When I found her," Olivia said, "she said something like, 'I heard them.' She must have heard noises, bad enough noises that she hid in the closet."

"I wonder what she heard. Words? Scuffling? Screams?"

"She wasn't specific." Olivia took a sip of her tea and sighed. "I think I need a shower. I just want to wash this whole night away."

"I don't know if I can sleep," Melissa said. "Even though I'm exhausted."

Olivia dumped her barely touched tea down the sink, rinsed the mug, and headed to the shower. When she came out and walked to her bedroom, she stopped short at the door. Melissa's petite body was lying on the floor in a sleeping bag next to Olivia's bed.

Melissa lifted her head from the pillow. "No way I'm sleeping alone in my room."

Olivia nodded. She took off her bathrobe and slipped under her blanket.

"Can we leave the light on?" Melissa asked.

"I was going to suggest the same thing," Olivia admitted.

Both young women closed their eyes, but neither one got much sleep. They were too alert, too focused on listening for any noise, like hushed footsteps or the click of a doorknob turning.

3

On Saturday, Olivia, Melissa, Colleen, and Ynes arranged to meet for lunch to talk about the events of the previous night. Colleen's parents were driving up from Connecticut and would arrive later in the afternoon to take her home. Melissa talked to her parents by phone and she planned to head back to western Massachusetts for a couple of days after meeting the others for lunch. Olivia made a call to her Aunt Aggie and Joe to tell them what had happened.

Aggie had raised Olivia from the age of one and Joe lived in the house next door to them in Ogunquit, Maine. He was like a dad to Olivia and had been there for her for the past twenty years. Until Olivia went off to college, Aggie and Olivia had lived in Cambridge and spent the weekends and summers in Maine. Aggie had recently retired from university teaching and the Ogunquit house was now her permanent residence.

Aggie and Joe were in Paris so that Aggie could attend an international law conference and when they heard what had happened in Somerville, they wanted to fly home immediately to be with Olivia.

"No, no," Olivia insisted. "I'm okay. I think it's better to just stick with my normal routine."

"I don't know, hon," Aggie told her. "I don't want you to be alone. We'll come home and we can all go back to Maine together. Maybe you should take the rest of the semester off."

"No way," Olivia said. "I'm graduating in May and I'm not letting this interfere with my plans. I'm not alone. My friends are around."

"Sweet pea," Joe said. He and Aggie were on speaker phone. "I think Aggie's right. This sort of thing can be hard to deal with. It can take a toll on you."

"If I have trouble dealing with things, then I'll call you. I promise. If I need you, you know I'll call. I won't suffer in silence." Olivia tried to lighten the mood. "You know I'm a wimp," she kidded.

"You are many things, and not all good, but...." Joe teased.

"Thanks a lot, Joe," Olivia interrupted him.

"But a wimp is not one of them," Joe finished his sentence.

Olivia smiled to herself. Joe always had a knack for

making her feel better. "I'll be okay. If I need to, I'll talk with one of the campus counselors."

"Go speak with them," Aggie said. "It might help you process the whole mess."

Joe said, "Don't be alone. Stay with your friends. Keep busy."

"I never have trouble keeping busy," Olivia told them. "I'll be okay."

"We'll come back if you want us to," Aggie said. "Just say the word, if you change your mind, and need a break from school...if you want to get away from there for a bit. Or, come here and visit Paris with us. Joe and I will pay for your ticket."

"We will?" Joe said in mock surprise.

"That's quite an offer," Olivia said. "But it's mid-semester. I don't want to jeopardize my credits. I want to graduate on time."

"I understand," Aggie said. "Call us anytime if you want to talk. Don't worry about the time difference. Let us know what's going on. And take care of yourself. Be sure to eat well and get rest." She hesitated a moment before saying, "Be careful, Liv. Be alert. Lock your doors. The killer is still at large."

"I'll be careful," Olivia said. "I promise."

"We love you," Joe said. "Call us if you need anything."

"I love you both. Don't worry." Olivia ended the call. Just hearing their voices made her feel less sad and unsettled, but a sense of loneliness suddenly tugged at her. She wished they were in Maine, because despite what she'd said, Olivia would have gone home for a few days to be with them. If she'd had some way of knowing what fate had in store and, that in six months, Aggie would be dead of a heart attack, Olivia would have flown to Paris to be with her dear aunt. Letting out a sigh, she went to her room to get ready to go out.

Olivia and Melissa left the apartment and walked to Davis Square where they caught the subway known as the "T" and rode to the Harvard University area of Cambridge. They walked down Massachusetts Ave to the restaurant where they would meet the other young women. The hostess ushered them to a booth near the window where Colleen was waiting.

Colleen had checked into a hotel in Harvard Square even though she had been invited by friends to stay with them. Completely devastated by her room-mates' murders, she was struggling with having been in the apartment while the crime was committed. She preferred to stay out of apartments for the time being and thought that hotels provided more security. Olivia didn't agree with that. She thought Colleen should be around friends, not staying alone in a hotel room, but she kept her opinion to herself.

Colleen had dark circles under her eyes and her face looked pale and gaunt. She had no makeup on and her auburn hair barely seemed brushed. It was a stark contrast from the way she usually looked, always so put together and polished. Olivia could see that Colleen was unraveling and it gave her a sinking feeling in her gut.

Colleen hugged Melissa and Olivia.

"How are you doing?" Melissa asked. She knew it was a lame question.

"I'm okay." Colleen picked at the paper napkin that was under her silverware. Her eyes flicked about the room like a hunted animal waiting for a predator to strike.

"Were you able to get any rest last night?" Olivia asked.

"Not much." Colleen shrugged. "I slept a few hours this morning. I think."

Olivia wanted to say something comforting, but didn't know what would help. "Your parents will be here soon."

Colleen nodded and as her eyes filled with tears, she blinked them away.

A waitress took drink orders just as Ynes came into the restaurant, spotted the girls and hurried over to the table. She sat next to Colleen and gave her a hug.

"Can you talk about it, Colleen?" Melissa's voice was gentle. "Can you tell us what happened?"

"I want to, yes." Colleen gave a slight nod.

"Were you in your room the whole time?" Olivia asked.

Colleen sipped from her water glass. She placed it back on the table, but kept her hand clenched around it. "I got home late from work. I showered, then went to my room to dry my hair. My door was shut. The hairdryer was on, so I didn't hear anything until I finished and turned it off."

"What happened after you turned off the hair dryer?" Ynes asked.

Colleen's eyes widened. For a moment, Olivia didn't think she was going to answer.

In a hushed tone she finally said, "I was in my room putting on makeup. I heard shouting. It was coming from the living room. At first, I thought the guys were joking or maybe had some sports thing on TV and were excited about whatever they were watching. But then, I don't know, the voices didn't sound right. I went closer to my door to listen. Something seemed wrong." She wrung her hands together and glanced down.

The others waited, not wanting to push Colleen.

"You don't need to tell us," Melissa said.

"I want to." Colleen sucked in a breath. "What I heard was over quick. Shouting. A scream." She clasped her hands together to try to conceal their shaking. "I heard some footsteps coming down the hall. I thought of pushing my desk chair up against the door. My room doesn't have a lock on it, but I was afraid to make any noise. I hurried over to the closet trying to be as quiet as I could. I got in and closed the door. I waited. I heard someone step into my room. I held my breath. I prayed that no one would come to get me. I almost passed out." She looked up. "After a while, Olivia opened the closet door."

"Did you hear Olivia call your name?" Ynes asked.

"No." Colleen turned her pale face to Olivia. "Did you call for me?"

"I think so," Olivia said. "I don't really remember."

"You did," Ynes told her. "I wondered why on earth you took off down the hall. I thought you were crazy. I worried the killer was still in the apartment. But, when you yelled for Colleen, I knew what you were doing."

"I was afraid you were hurt," Olivia said to Colleen.

"That's when you saw the killer in the hall," Ynes said.

"You saw him?" Colleen's voice was thin and high-pitched.

Olivia nodded. "I saw someone. I don't know if it was the killer."

"Who the heck else could it have been?" Melissa asked.

"I was just thinking. Maybe, it was someone coming to the party," Olivia said. "Couldn't they have come up the back staircase? It just jumped into my mind that it could have been someone else. Couldn't it have just been another person coming to the party?"

They sat in silence, thinking.

"But, he had a ski mask on," Melissa said.

"It could have been his costume," Ynes said. "We all had some Halloween thing on."

"Why did he run then?" Melissa asked.

"Fear? Afraid to be blamed for the deaths? Not knowing who we were? He could have been scared by what he heard and took off," Olivia said. "I don't think we can assume he was the killer."

"It's certainly possible that who you saw in the hallway was just a party-goer," Ynes said. "Or," she hesitated. "Maybe it was the killer."

They considered the possibilities.

"So maybe you didn't see the murderer at all." Melissa looked at Olivia and breathed out a sigh of relief. "That makes me feel better. I worried he might come after you."

"A guy who was at the party, Jack something," Olivia said. "He told us he was smoking at the back door of the apartment that night. He said he saw two people wearing ski masks leave the building."

"Two people?" Ynes asked. "Together?"

Olivia shook her head. "Jack said they didn't seem to be together. They left the building at different times."

"How can we find out who these people in the ski masks are?" Melissa asked.

"I don't think we can find out," Ynes said. She

looked at Olivia. "Did you tell the police you saw someone in the hallway?"

Olivia nodded. "Yeah, I told them, but there wasn't much to say. I couldn't see enough to give a very accurate description."

"What could have been the motive?" Ynes addressed the question to Colleen. "Were the guys into anything that would put them in danger?" Olivia asked. "Did

they have enemies?"

Colleen shook her head. "No." Her shoulders slumped. "I don't know. Why would anyone do this?"

"Did either one of them mention trouble with someone? A run-in with anybody? Online harassment?" Olivia pressed, trying to think of any little thing that could lead to finding the person who killed Gary and Christian.

"No," Colleen said. "I never heard about any trouble."

"How about at work?" Olivia asked. "What about Gary? Did he have any trouble with a student? A parent? Did either of them ever mention a clash with a co-worker?"

"No." Colleen's eyes filled with tears. "Christian got along with the people he worked with. He was moving out of our apartment on the first of November. He wanted to be closer to work, wanted to be able to walk to work. He was moving in with a friend of his from

MIT, Luke Smithson." She rubbed at her forehead. "Gary loved his job. He loved the kids he worked with. He never complained about anything."

"You said your bedroom door was shut when you heard the commotion, when you hid in the closet," Olivia said. "You heard your bedroom door open when you were hiding?"

Colleen nodded.

"The killer must have opened the door," Melissa said.

Colleen winced.

"Did you hear any voices when you heard the bedroom door open?" Olivia asked.

"No. I didn't hear any talking." Colleen's face scrunched up trying to hold back her tears. "Why would someone do this?" she whispered. "Why?"

MELISSA AND OLIVIA decided to walk back to their Somerville apartment thinking that maybe the crisp, fall air would help to clear their heads.

"I'm exhausted," Melissa said. "I barely slept. All night I kept listening for noises in the apartment."

"Me, too. Every little squeak or branch blowing in the wind had me jumping."

"What do you think about the murders, Liv?"

"I don't know what to think. Maybe it was random,

some crazy person, maybe somebody high on something. He got in, went nuts." She shoved her hands into her jacket pockets. "Or maybe it was planned."

"I can't stand thinking about it anymore. The police will figure it out."

"Maybe we should talk to the guy Christian was planning to move in with. Luke Smith?" Olivia said.

"Smithson," Melissa told her.

"Maybe he knows if Christian had an enemy or had a fight with someone."

"That's a good idea. We should wait a few days to contact him though. He must be so upset," Melissa said. "Are you sure you don't want to come home with me for a couple of days? Get away from here?"

"I'll be okay. I have a lot of work to do. I'll be busy, but, thanks." Olivia wasn't looking forward to being in the apartment alone while Melissa went home, but she was feeling so frazzled she didn't want to have to make small talk with people she barely knew. And anyway, she had so much to catch up on that she hoped work could distract her from the horror of the previous night.

She also knew that was a ridiculous idea.

4

Olivia sat hunched over her laptop reading and editing the essay she'd been working on for over three hours. The words swam on the screen and she leaned back and blinked several times trying to clear her vision. She rubbed at her temples where an achy tingle pulsed under the skin.

Checking the clock, Olivia was surprised at the late hour and that the time had flown by so fast. She hadn't intended to stay that long in the library.

Leaning back to stretch her shoulder and neck muscles, a gnawing sensation in her stomach made her realize she hadn't eaten anything for hours. Olivia shut down her laptop, closed up her notebooks, and pushed everything into her backpack.

Melissa had gone back to her parents' home for two nights to be with her family. Some of Olivia's friends had texted inviting her to dinner or to meet for drinks later, but she was looking forward to relaxing in her apartment and maybe watching a movie in her pajamas. Images of last night's murder victims had unexpectedly flashed into her head throughout the day, and she didn't feel like acting upbeat or jovial. She just wanted to take some time for a long bath and turn in early after her day of studying.

Olivia flung her backpack over her shoulder and stepped into the dark, cool October night. The wind tossed dried leaves around the sidewalk as she made her way down the hill to the streets that would lead to her apartment. Last night's events started playing through her mind, and as she walked, she pulled her jacket closer around her body. She tried to think of other things to distract herself from reliving the discovery of the dead bodies and the gruesome scene in the apartment. Picturing herself summer kayaking in the river behind Ogunquit beach in Maine, she smiled remembering the icy water splashing on her sun-baked skin as she paddled. Olivia loved the water, whether sailing on the Charles River, or boogie boarding or kayaking in the ocean. When she was little, Aggie and Joe called her a fish because they could never get her out of the water.

Olivia turned left onto a tree-lined, side street. Two streetlights were out and the sidewalk was black. She slowed her pace so that she wouldn't stumble over anything. No one was around, the area was deserted. The moon and the stars were hidden by heavy cloud cover.

Olivia started to feel a prickle of apprehension, and despite being chilled by the cold breeze, a drop of sweat trickled down her back. She heard the rustle of footsteps behind her, but wasn't sure if she was imagining it since her feet scrunching on the dry leaves muffled any other sounds. The weird and sudden sensation that someone's eyes were on her back made her heartbeat speed up. Primitive instinct set off alarm bells in her head that danger lurked somewhere on the street.

Olivia picked up her pace. She fought the urge to turn her head to look back, afraid to alert whoever was following that she was aware of his presence.

Should she run? If someone *was* behind her, watching her, if she ran, would that make the person following her become aggressive? Should she stay alert and just keep quickening her pace? *Why is my apartment not closer to campus?*

Although Olivia didn't want to indicate by glancing around that she was suspicious that someone was following her, she needed to convince herself that she was safe, so she stopped, bent down, and pretended to be fixing her shoe to try to get a look behind.

Out of the corner of her eye, Olivia saw someone on the sidewalk stop and step into the shadow of an apartment house. Her breath hitched in her throat and her stomach lurched. She tried to squash the panic flooding her veins. *Get a hold of yourself. Think.*

She stood and hurried to the other side of the street, listening closely for any sounds behind her. Pulling her phone from her jacket pocket, she pressed the keys for 911 as she walked, but didn't send the call. She transferred the phone into her left hand and grasped her keys in her right, placing one key between each finger.

If anyone tried to grab her, she would press the button to send the emergency call and slash at the attacker's face with the keys.

Olivia attempted to settle her breathing by adjusting her intake of air with long slow breaths. She listened for the sound of someone gaining on her, but the pounding of blood in her ears blocked out any indication of movement behind her.

I know he's there. I can feel his eyes on me.

Almost to the corner of her street, she decided she would bolt for her building after rounding the turn. If she screamed, maybe someone inside would hear her.

Three more steps, two more. Olivia sprinted to the apartment and tore up the stairs to the front porch where she plunged her keys into the lock and yanked the door open. Inside, she slammed it shut with her body's full force and turned the lock. She stood facing the door, gasping.

"Liv." A man's voice spoke behind her.

Olivia whirled.

Her first floor neighbor stood next to her. "You okay? Is the devil chasing you or something?" he joked.

She collected herself and gave him a half-smile. "Maybe. It's almost Halloween, you know."

Breathing hard, Olivia started up the stairs to her apartment. Reaching the sixth floor, she unlocked her door, stepped inside, and slid the bolt and chain into place. She entered the apartment without turning on any lights, slipped the backpack off her shoulder, and hurried to the front window to look out at the black street. Pressing against the wall, she tilted her head to peer outside. Her eyes searched up and down, but she only saw her neighbor making his way up the road. Her hands trembled.

I know you're out there. I felt you. What do you want?

5

The sun's rays slipped through the sides of Olivia's window shade and illuminated her bedroom with bright, October morning light. She'd been jittery all evening, keeping only one interior light on and staying away from the apartment windows so no one on the sidewalk below could see her moving about inside.

She had planned on ordering take-out to be delivered, but decided against having to open the door to a deliveryman. Instead, she pulled out flour and baking soda, measured it into a glass bowl, and added a little salt, some oil, and water. She mixed it together and kneaded it for a few minutes on the counter.

Olivia roasted broccoli and cauliflower with some garlic and when it was done, she covered the pizza dough with sauce and some grated cheese, and topped it with the roasted vegetables. After a short time in the oven, the apartment filled with the mouth-watering aroma of baking pizza.

Olivia was no gourmet cook, but she knew her way around the kitchen having learned from Joe and Aggie. The three of them would often cook together or take turns making dinner to give each other a break from food preparation. Olivia decided at the age of ten to become a vegetarian and she concocted many dishes that even meat lovers like Aggie and Joe enjoyed.

She also discovered that cooking sometimes helped to calm her when she was having a problem or that it aided in clearing her head when she needed to think something through.

Last night she needed to focus on making dinner not only because she was starving, but because she needed to keep busy to channel her nervous energy into something besides pacing around the apartment and worrying.

Eating her pizza with a salad while she sat in front of her laptop with a movie playing, she couldn't pay attention to the storyline and turned it off. Olivia would have loved to have gone for a run, but that was out of the question.

All evening, she kept sidling up to the window to peer out at the street. Nothing looked suspicious and she started to think that maybe she'd imagined that someone was following her along the sidewalk. Even so, her worry kept her from taking the long bath that she had planned, not wanting to be in the bathroom tub if someone broke into the apartment. It was foolish to think that way and she even chuckled at herself, but still … she decided on a quick shower instead, which wasn't such a great idea either because all she could picture while lathering and rinsing was the shower scene from *Psycho.*

Olivia ended her evening by putting on her pajamas and crawling into bed, leaving the small lamp on her dresser lit all night. She wished Melissa was back from her visit home.

After stretching to get the kinks out of her back, she crawled out of bed and went to the kitchen to eat a banana. The day was so bright and cheery and she was itching with excess energy so she put on exercise clothes, grabbed her keys and phone, and stepped outside into the crisp air. Perfect weather for a run.

Olivia wasn't fast, but she could run for long distances. Not long after leaving her apartment and jogging down several streets, her muscles warmed and she settled into a comfortable pace as she made her way from Somerville through Cambridge and back again completing an eight-mile circuit. The exercise calmed her mind and pushed the images of the Friday night murders out of her thoughts. Feeling more like herself, she believed that being hyped up about the killings had contributed to her imagining being followed the previous night.

Her phone vibrated with an incoming text from Melissa. *Decided to come back this evening. Let's go out for dinner tonight and talk.*

Relief at having Melissa back and not having to be alone in the apartment flooded Olivia's body and she answered with a "yes!" They agreed to go to Davis Square at 7pm after Melissa returned from her family home in Stockbridge.

Finishing her run, Olivia felt energized. She showered and dressed and ate a snack before leaving to meet the two middle-school students she'd volunteered to tutor in math twice a week.

Before heading out, she opened her laptop to look at the news of the day. An article discussing the Friday night murders caught her eye and her heart thudded hard. She debated ignoring the article, but couldn't do it. The story reported that two university students had discovered the bodies around 10pm on Friday evening, but the article did not name them. *At least they didn't mention our names.*

Olivia did not want her name in the news article. She didn't want to be linked to the events of that night and hoped to stay anonymous. She and Melissa thought it best not to alert the killer to who they were, but Olivia wondered how long it would take the media to print their names in upcoming stories.

The report had pictures of the young men, both smiling and looking happy and confident in their photos. They were just two young guys starting their lives, eager and optimistic about their futures. Olivia's heart squeezed. *How did this happen?*

The article continued with short biographies of the dead men. Christian Wilcox, a native of Connecticut, had graduated from MIT with a degree in computer science and engineering and had been working at a start-up in Cambridge's Kendall Square area. Christian was a nationally ranked tennis player and had been active in several college clubs.

Gary Sullivan had grown up in the same Connecticut town and attended high school with Christian. Gary graduated last May from Boston University with a degree in education and math and was employed as a teacher in an inner city school. The young man had been on the track team and held several university records in the 5K and 10K distances. Working with disadvantaged young people had been Gary's dream and he was thrilled to be starting his career.

The article mentioned that a roommate who was home at the time of the murders had escaped injury.

Olivia looked up and stared off into space. Gary and Christian sounded like two normal, accomplished young men.

Why would someone want them dead?

6

A fter her session tutoring the students, Olivia headed for the library where she was going to meet Ynes. Ynes had texted Olivia asking to get together to talk about the killings. As Olivia followed the sidewalk leading to the front door of the library, she spotted Ynes coming down the hill towards her. They greeted each other and entered the library, choosing one of the study rooms off the main lobby for privacy. Inside the small room there was a large desk and two cushioned chairs. Before sitting down, Ynes closed the door.

"I can't stop thinking about the crime," Olivia said. "Even though I'd never met the guys, I feel connected to the murders because we found the bodies."

"I understand." Ynes slowly shook her head. "I only knew Gary slightly. It's just so unbelievable. I haven't been able to sleep very much." Ynes had grown up in London and her voice carried an English accent. She brushed her long, wavy, black hair away from her eyes. "The whole thing is just so terrible."

Olivia nodded. "Melissa went home for a couple of days. I was alone last night. I can't keep the images of the bodies from flashing in my mind. I think about who could have done it," she said. "Do you think the killer knew Gary and Christian?"

"I can't believe it was random," Ynes said. "They lived on the second floor. If someone was randomly looking to kill someone, why would he choose that building? That floor? I don't think it could have been by chance. I think someone deliberately sought them out."

"What do you know about Gary?" Olivia asked.

"That's what I wanted to talk to you about. Gary was a teacher. He graduated last May. Like I said, I didn't know him well at all. But I know someone who did know him. Her name is Eva Flores. She works at her brother's gym in Revere. Gary used to work out there."

"What did she say about Gary?" Olivia asked.

"Eva had gone out with Gary a few times. She told me there are some tough characters who hang out at this gym. One of them had a thing for Eva. She went out with this guy once, but didn't like him and wouldn't see him again. He was always pressuring her to go out with him and he didn't like that Eva had started seeing Gary."

When Ynes paused, Olivia asked, "Did something happen between Gary and that guy?"

"It sure did. Eva said the guy and his friend showed up at a club one night when she was out with Gary. The guys approached them and tried to make trouble. One of them took a swing at Gary, but Gary ducked and punched the guy in the face. The bouncer saw the whole thing and kicked the two idiots out of the place. Eva said the guy cursed at Gary and told him that he better start looking over his shoulder because he was a dead man."

Olivia's eyes were wide. "Do you know when this happened?"

"Yes. The weekend before Gary and Christian were killed."

"Oh, no." Olivia looked around the small room, her mind racing. "Did your friend report this to the police?"

"She's afraid to," Ynes said, her voice just above a whisper. "Eva says this guy is big-time trouble. She is terrified of him."

"Did she tell you his name?"

"Adam Johnson. He's a semi-pro football player. Eva says there's gossip about him being involved in some really nasty stuff. She says he beat up a former girlfriend, but the girl wouldn't press charges. There's some talk of him being involved in a couple of murders. Drugs, too. Eva won't go to the police. She's afraid he'll kill her."

"Kill her? We should tell the police that he threatened Gary," Olivia said. "We can leave Eva's name out of it."

"I don't think so." Ynes shook her head. "He'd suspect Eva reported it."

"What about an anonymous tip?" Olivia asked.

"He'd still think Eva talked to the police. Eva says that Johnson or one of his goons is always watching her. They follow her places. Eva's brother is afraid of this guy, too. He'd like him out of his gym, but he knows he can't do anything to make him leave."

"Really? What do you think?" Olivia asked. "Is there some way we could tip off the police to this information without putting your friend at risk?"

Ynes shrugged. "I haven't been able to think of a way. I wanted to talk it over with you."

Olivia sat back in her seat trying to think of a way to pass the information to the police and keep Eva out of it. "What if we say we were at the club that night? That we saw the fight? We heard the threat that Johnson made to Gary."

"Then Johnson will come after us."

"But how would he find out we were the ones who came forward?" Olivia asked.

Ynes sat quietly for several seconds, her face serious. "From what Eva says about this Johnson guy, it worries me to get involved. She says he acts like he's above the law. I don't trust many people, Olivia. I've had some experiences that make me very cautious. What if this guy has connections, maybe with someone in law enforcement? Or what if he knows someone who has a friend in law enforcement? What if he has guys who will do whatever he tells them to do? Do you want to take the chance? If he killed Gary and Christian, do you think he'd hesitate to kill us?"

Olivia let out a sigh. With her elbow on the table, she placed her chin in her hand trying to think of a way to get the information to the police.

Ynes went on. "Eva and her brother would like to see if Johnson has something stashed in his gym locker that could implicate him for some crime ... a weapon, or some evidence that linked him to a murder, something that could get him arrested. Anything that would get him out of their lives. They'd love to check the trunk of his car, too, but they know that's too risky. Eva asked me if I would look at Johnson's locker. She won't do it. Neither will her brother. She says Johnson monitors them all the time. It's like he's stalking Eva. She can't look at the locker when the gym is open because of all the people around. She won't stay there after hours because she doesn't want to risk being alone there and having Johnson come in. Johnson has a key to the gym."

Olivia sat up. "Why does he?"

Ynes furrowed her brow and gave a shrug. "Eva's brother gave it to him. Johnson isn't a guy you say no to."

"Eva thinks Johnson killed Gary and Christian?"

"She thinks it's possible, given the talk around Johnson and because of the threat he made to Gary." Ynes sat back in the chair looking defeated. "Eva would love to have Johnson put away and if he has a weapon or something incriminating in his locker, well, then maybe it would be worth calling the police about that."

"Could she get a restraining order against Johnson? If he's always after her, isn't that grounds for such a thing? Wouldn't the courts help her?"

Ynes shook her head. "Eva says that she's never heard of a restraining order that helped anyone. She's afraid if she does something like that, it would just inflame Johnson."

"Would he keep a weapon in his locker? If he did murder the guys, he must have dumped the knife somewhere," Olivia said.

"Who knows? Maybe he isn't careful." Ynes leveled her eyes at Olivia, her face somber, and didn't say anything.

Olivia straightened in her seat. "You want me to help you, don't you?"

"Maybe." Worry or sadness tugged at Ynes' face.

Olivia couldn't determine which emotion it was that suddenly made her friend look a few years older.

"If we decide to check it out," Olivia said, "Eva could let us into the gym after hours?"

"Yes. That's the idea," Ynes said. "I'm not sure yet if it's a good one."

Olivia leaned forward. "What about his car? Johnson could have something in the trunk. What if we broke into it while he was at the gym or wherever he hangs out?"

Ynes gaped at Olivia. "Do you know how to break into a trunk?"

"How hard could it be? There are probably instructions on the internet," Olivia said. "Although, it's probably larceny or something if we break into a trunk? I don't want to end up in jail."

"We'll probably end up *in* his trunk. Dead." Ynes said, "I'm starting to worry that your sense of self-preservation isn't intact."

"Oh, it is," Olivia said. "But someone killed Gary and Christian. Melissa and I found the bodies. I know I'll never get that image out of my head. It's seared into my brain cells. And, your friend, she must be living in constant fear of this Johnson guy." Olivia sighed. "A monster like this shouldn't be able to torment people or walk around living his life after robbing Gary and Christian of their lives. If there's something we can do to figure out who killed them, or if we can help your friend, then I think we should try. Maybe we could find something that would get Johnson away from your friend."

Olivia inhaled a long breath and let it out. "If we don't find anything on this Johnson guy, at least we gave it a shot. Aren't we smarter than he is, Ynes? If we decide to look at his locker or at his car, I don't intend for us to get caught." Olivia narrowed her eyes. "And if we do get caught, well, I guess we'll just have to outwit him."

"Okay." A slight smile formed over Ynes' lips and she nodded. "Let's try the locker. I'll talk to Eva. Maybe she can get us a key to the gym. We could go there when it's closed. We can get in, check out Johnson's locker, and get out fast."

"Let me know what Eva says. The sooner we can check this out, the better."

7

Olivia returned to her apartment taking the same route that she'd walked the previous night, but this time she wasn't spooked thinking that someone was following her. Feeling safer probably had to do with the fact that there were people walking in the area so Olivia wasn't alone and it wasn't fully dark yet.

Melissa had returned home thirty minutes earlier and texted Olivia announcing her arrival. When Olivia reached the landing outside their apartment, the door flew open and Melissa wrapped her in a hug.

They entered the apartment and Olivia halted in her tracks when she saw what was on the coffee table. "What the heck is that?"

"Exactly what it looks like." Melissa picked up a red

handled axe and held it menacingly at Olivia. "I brought it from home."

"Melissa, no," Olivia said. "Someone will just use it on us."

"I'm keeping it in my room ... just in case." She lowered the axe and leaned it next to the sofa. "Have you been following the news reports?" Melissa asked.

"Yes. They haven't reported our names yet."

"Well, they just did. It's in that rag of a newspaper, the *Courier*. We ought to sue them," Melissa said. "Or use the axe on them."

Olivia was not pleased that their names were in the paper in connection with the killings. "Did they say anything else about us except our names?"

"'University students.' But they didn't say which university ... yet. It won't take much time before some stupid reporter puts us at risk by telling other facts about us."

"Is this why you came back early?" Olivia asked.

Melissa plopped onto the sofa. "No. If I knew our names were in the paper, I might have stayed home for a while longer." She clutched a pillow to her chest. "I just wanted to be here with you. My parents were so concerned for me, it made me feel weird and unsafe. I want to be able to talk about it sometimes, but I feel like I'll just upset them. I wanted to come back and talk with you."

"I'm glad you came back," Olivia said. She told Melissa about her conversation with Ynes.

"Oh, Liv. I don't know. That guy sounds very dangerous. It might be too risky."

Olivia said, "There's something else." She told Melissa how she had the distinct sensation that someone was following her home last night.

Melissa sat up straight, her forehead creased with worry. "So what do you think today? Was it your imagination?"

Olivia shrugged. "I'd like it to be."

"Oh, no." Melissa stood, went to the windows, and pulled the cord at each of the front bay windows to lower the blinds. "I wish this apartment was in the back of the building." She turned to Olivia. "Should we call the police?"

"Let's see if it happens again," Olivia told her.

Melissa moaned.

"Come on," Olivia said. "Let's go eat. Maybe we'll get followed on the way home and we can jump the guy and take him out."

"Why did I come back?" Melissa picked up her jacket from the chair and muttered, "Why didn't I just stay home?"

∼

OLIVIA AND MELISSA headed down College Avenue towards the area of restaurants and shops where they planned to have dinner. As they passed apartment buildings and a convenience store, a young man who had just parked his car along the street, stepped out of it and onto the sidewalk. It was Jack, the young guy who had arrived outside of Gary and Christian's apartment around the time Olivia and Melissa found the bodies.

Melissa called to him. "Hey, Jack."

"How are you?" Olivia asked. "We're going to dinner if you want to come."

When they got closer, the young women could see that the left side of Jack's face near his jawline was swollen and full.

"I've got a tooth abscess so I'll pass," he told them. "I've got a dentist appointment tomorrow morning. Another time, though."

"Can we get you anything?" Olivia asked.

"I'll be all right," Jack said.

"How are you doing?" Melissa asked. "Since, the murders?"

"Okay. Mostly."

"If you ever want to get together and talk, it might be good for all of us," Melissa offered.

"That's probably a good idea." Jack put his hand to his jaw. "I'm going in and going to bed."

"Hope you feel better," Olivia said.

The girls wished him luck with the dental

appointment and continued down the hill. They walked into Davis Square, and as they passed an Irish pub, one of their friends called to them and invited the girls to join them inside for a drink. They agreed and stood at the bar with five friends from the university.

The bar was crowded with young people and neighborhood residents enjoying an Irish band playing their original rock-infused traditional songs. The group of friends ordered several appetizers, chatted with each other, and clapped along to the music. After two hours, Olivia and Melissa excused themselves and strolled through the busy square to a different pub for dinner. Tiny white lights were strung along the branches of the trees that lined the main street and warm golden light spilled from the windows of eateries and pubs. Pumpkins, mums, and cornstalks decorated doorways and window boxes.

"That was fun," Melissa said, "and only Mike brought up the murders."

"I was glad the topic shifted to other things so fast and we didn't have to dwell on the killings," Olivia said.

"I don't think any of them even knew we were at the apartment that night," Melissa said.

"Mike knows we were there, but he doesn't know we were the ones who found the bodies. He asked me about it, but I said we didn't see much," Olivia said. "I left it at that. I didn't say we were first on the scene."

"Good thinking. They mustn't have seen the news article reporting our names."

"It won't take long before that bit of news starts circulating," Olivia said.

The girls entered the pub and were seated in a back booth. They ordered iced teas and entrees and chatted about their classes and graduate school applications. When the meals came, they dug in with gusto. They planned to watch a movie together when they got home, but couldn't decide which one to pick.

"Something light. Maybe, a comedy?" Melissa suggested.

Before Olivia could reply, both of their phones buzzed with incoming text messages and they lifted the phones to see who was contacting them.

"A university text and another one from Ynes," Olivia said as she bent closer to read the messages on the screen in the darkly lit pub.

"Same," Melissa said as she read her texts.

Olivia's blue eyes went wide and her pulse started to race. When she looked across the table at Melissa, she could see her friend's hand shaking as she held her phone in front of her eyes.

"Jack," Olivia said. The word choked her. Her eyes misted over and she had to swallow hard to speak.

"Someone killed him," Melissa said, her voice trembling. "Why is this happening?" Panic sparked in her eyes. "What's going on? Who's doing it?"

THE GIRLS PAID for their meals, rushed out of the pub, and ran up College Avenue to Jack's building. The police cars' blue lights flashed against the houses and people gathered in small clusters across the street. Police radios squawked snippets of conversations that were impossible to make out.

Olivia and Melissa scanned the groups and found a few friends standing together staring at the building that Jack had called home. Ynes was with them.

"What have you heard?" Olivia asked her.

"I found out about it from texts and tweets that went out," Ynes told her. "I thought you'd want to know." Her face looked pinched and tired. "We haven't heard much."

"Was he stabbed?"

Ynes nodded. "That's what people are saying. Just like Gary and Christian." Her fingers shook as she nervously brushed her long hair behind her ears.

A young man they knew stepped closer. "Jessie found him. He was at the bottom of the stairs." Jessie was Jack's girlfriend.

Olivia and Melissa exchanged a look. "If they found him at the bottom of the steps," Olivia whispered, "the killer must have attacked right after we talked to Jack." She shuddered, feeling light-headed.

"The killer must have been right here. He must

have seen us talking to Jack." Melissa's voice sounded strained.

"If we had taken him to dinner, he'd still be alive." Olivia brushed at the tears that were threatening to fall.

Melissa slipped her arm through Olivia's. Olivia could feel her friend shaking next to her.

"Do you remember anyone nearby when we were talking to Jack?" Olivia asked.

Melissa tried to recall. "People walked by us and I think people were on the opposite sidewalk, but no one stands out."

"I didn't notice anything out of the ordinary, either." Olivia watched the officials buzzing in and out of the apartment building. She thought of Jack's girlfriend finding him. "Poor Jessie."

"Poor Jack," Melissa added.

"We need to tell the police we saw him earlier this evening," Olivia said.

"Just wait a few minutes before we go over. I can't do it right now."

Olivia nodded and scanned the ever-increasing crowd. Students, young professionals, neighbors, a few little kids. Everyone stood in small clusters, speaking in hushed tones.

As Olivia's gaze traveled over the people, her eyes passed a lone person standing off the sidewalk at the corner, in the gutter of the road under the streetlight. It was a slender woman about Olivia's age. She had spikey, short blonde hair and was dressed in jeans and a fitted brown leather jacket. Her hands were shoved into her pockets.

Something seemed familiar about her and Olivia flicked her eyes back to the woman. The blonde had turned her body to face Olivia and her eyes stared across the crowd like lasers. Olivia looked at the woman trying to place her, wondering if she should acknowledge her by waving.

An unmarked police car tore up College Avenue with its siren blaring. It halted in front of Jack's building.

Olivia turned and nudged Melissa. "Do you know that girl? Over there near the side street?"

"Where? Who?" Melissa craned her neck.

Olivia looked back to the corner. The girl was gone. Her eyes swept the crowd, but she couldn't locate the young woman.

"Where is she?" Melissa asked.

"I don't see her anymore. She must have left."

"Why do you ask about her? Who is she?"

"I don't know. She seemed familiar. She was staring at me for a minute. I felt uncomfortable. I thought I should wave or nod or something, but then I wondered if she was looking at someone next to us."

"Maybe that's what she was doing. Maybe it just seemed like she was looking at you."

"Maybe. It seemed like she was staring at me though." Olivia examined the crowd again to see if she could locate the girl, but she didn't see her anywhere. Olivia felt slightly uneasy because of what seemed like the blonde's attention on her, but she couldn't understand why it was so unnerving. She took a deep breath and tried to shake off the feeling.

Olivia and Melissa crossed to the other side of the street and when they saw a woman police officer head to her cruiser, they approached and told the law enforcement official their names and that they had seen Jack several hours ago. They also reported they'd been the ones to discover the murdered bodies of Christian and Gary. The officer took down the information and then the two friends returned to where they'd been standing on the other side of the street.

People had begun to disperse. Ynes stepped away from the students she was with and moved next to Olivia and Melissa.

"Did the officer tell you anything?" Ynes asked.

Olivia shook her head. "We saw Jack earlier tonight. We passed his car when he was parking it. We asked him to join us for dinner."

"Obviously, he didn't," Ynes said sadly.

Olivia shook her head again.

"It freaks me out," Melissa said. "The killer must have been watching the building. He must have seen the three of us talking." Her eyes flashed with worry. "What if the killer comes after us? What if we're next?"

"I don't think so," Ynes said. "It's only guys that are getting killed. So it seems."

Melissa stared at her. "You think so?"

"It seems like that … so far, anyway, the killer has only targeted men."

Olivia processed Ynes' words. "You think the killer knows the guys? Has some sort of vendetta against them?"

"Who knows," Ynes said. "Maybe it's someone who has a view of the world that these guys don't fit into." Her words were laced with disgust.

Olivia spoke softly. "If the killer is that football player, Adam Johnson, why would he kill Jack?"

"Maybe because Jack was outside Gary and Christian's apartment right after they were killed?" Ynes suggested.

"The killer must have seen Jack smoking outside the building or passed him on the staircase when he was fleeing from the crime scene. But how would the killer know who Jack was? How could he find Jack so easily?" Olivia asked.

Ynes said, "The killer must have thought that Jack could identify him, so he killed him to silence him. I wonder if the killer did know Jack. He found out where Jack lived, at least." Some people called to Ynes before Olivia or Melissa could reply. "I'm going home," she said. "I'll give you a call, Olivia. We can decide if we should pay a visit to that gym I told you about." Ynes gave Olivia and Melissa's arms a squeeze. "Hopefully the police will figure this out and arrest someone."

"Will they?" Olivia asked no one in particular.

"Maybe," Melissa asked. "How soon though?"

"Not soon enough," Olivia said.

"Liv, do you think the killer knew Jack?" Melissa asked. "That scares me. What else does the killer know? *Who* else does the killer know? Us?"

Olivia's brow creased with worry. "The thought that the killer knows us scares me to death. But even if the killer does know some of us, what's the motive? Why is he killing them? Understanding that is the key to this whole thing."

"Well, the cops better figure it out. And they better find the suspect fast before this lunatic can kill someone else." Melissa pulled gloves out of her pockets and put them on.

Deciding to leave, the young women followed the side streets back to their apartment house. As they approached the front porch, Olivia looked over her shoulder. "At least nobody followed us home."

"Ugh. Don't even joke. I can't take it."

After unlocking the front door, they trudged up the stairs to the sixth floor.

"Why is there no elevator?" Melissa groaned as she led the way.

"Put that on your wish list for your next place," Olivia told her.

Melissa pulled her key out to unlock the apartment door. "What's this?"

"What?" Olivia looked over her friend's shoulder.

Melissa reached for something hanging on the doorknob. When she realized what it was, she screamed and flung the thing down the hallway.

Adrenaline shot through Olivia's body. "What is it?"

"Look!" Melissa wailed. "Look what it is!"

Olivia inched towards what Melissa had thrown down. As she bent and reached to lift it from the floor, her heart plummeted into her stomach.

A black, ski mask.

8

"**D**rop it, Liv," Melissa howled. "Don't touch it."

"It's okay. Let's go inside and check it out." Olivia tried to calm Melissa by keeping her voice steady and even, but her heart pounded like a sledge-hammer. She scanned the hallway as she herded Melissa back towards their door.

Fumbling with the key, Melissa pushed the door open to let Olivia enter first. "Wait." She grabbed Olivia's arm and yanked her back. "What if someone's inside?" she whispered.

"If someone's inside, they probably wouldn't warn us by hanging a ski mask on the doorknob." Olivia spoke softly just in case someone *was* inside. Standing at the threshold, she reached to find the switch pad to flick on the overhead lights. She stepped into the bright room, her nerves on high alert.

"Let's check the other rooms." Melissa spoke in a hushed tone, her body practically rammed up against Olivia's back.

When they entered the small kitchen, Melissa picked up a steak knife from the counter.

Olivia eyed it. "Not sure that will help," she said softly. She worried that someone might grab the knife from Melissa's hand and turn it on them.

"Better than what you're holding," Melissa whispered. Olivia still gripped the ski mask in her right hand.

They inched down the hall, Melissa close behind Olivia, holding the knife in one hand and clutching her friend's shoulder with the other. They peeked into the bathroom, pushed back the shower curtain, and then entered each bedroom and checked the closets and under the beds. Melissa breathed a sigh of relief.

They returned to the living room where Melissa pulled all the shades down. The nighttime task was becoming a habit. "We should turn the lights off so no one can see us from the street." She held the knife out in front of her.

"We can't just sit here in the dark every night," Olivia told her friend. "I think you can probably put the knife down now."

Melissa's shoulders started to shake. "You're still holding that stupid ski mask."

Olivia turned the knitted mask over in her hands and looked inside. "I was hoping there might be a note or something pinned to it."

"Should we call the police?" Melissa moved away from the windows.

"Maybe," Olivia said. "But...."

"But, what?"

"What are we going to say?" Oliva's voice held a tone of hopelessness. "We found a ski mask? Then they'll ask if it came with mittens, too."

"Ugh." Melissa groaned and as she walked to the coffee table to place the knife down, a loud knock sounded on the apartment door. Olivia whirled and Melissa let out a yelp. They both stood wide-eyed staring at the door.

Olivia swallowed. "Who is it?" She could barely squeak out the words.

Melissa picked up the knife with a trembling hand.

"Who's there?" Olivia asked again.

The two women shuffled to the door straining to hear. Olivia was about to place her eye up to the peep-hole, when her friend pulled her back and shook her head. Melissa raised her hand, her finger pointed like a gun and gestured at Olivia's eye.

A knock sounded. The girls jumped.

Melissa mimed opening the door. Olivia nodded,

took the knife from Melissa, and flattened herself against the wall. The chain was in place on the door. Melissa indicated she would open it just a crack to see who was there.

Olivia decided that if someone tried to force his way in, she would push the ski mask onto his face and plunge the knife into the hollow of his throat. She grimaced at the thought of doing such a thing, but held tight to the knife in her hand, looked at Melissa, and nodded. Melissa unlocked the bolt and opened the door a crack.

"No one," Melissa whispered. She raised her hand to remove the chain.

"No." Olivia placed her hand on Melissa's arm. "Let's not open it any wider. Someone might be hoping we step into the hall."

Melissa shut and locked the door and ignored her own advice by putting her eye up against the peephole. "I don't see anyone." She stepped back. "Is someone playing a prank?"

Olivia sidled to the door, looked through the peephole, and startled back. Someone stood in front of the door with a hand raised to knock again.

Leaning close to Melissa, Olivia whispered, "It's that girl from outside Jack's building."

"What girl?"

"The blonde who was staring at me." Olivia faced the door and demanded, "Who's there?"

"I need to talk," a woman's voice spoke from the other side of the door.

"Who are you?"

"I was a friend of Christian's."

Olivia and Melissa stood in silence, blinking at each other, unsure of what to do.

"I saw you at the guys' apartment." The voice paused. "The night of the murders. I was wearing the ski mask."

Olivia yanked the door open.

"Can I come in?" the blonde asked.

"I have a knife," Olivia warned.

"Me, too," Melissa blurted, even though she didn't have one.

"I didn't kill them," the blonde said. She was fine boned, about Olivia's height, with high cheekbones and skin like porcelain. Her blue eyes, fringed with long black lashes, were mesmerizing.

Something about the young woman made Olivia step back so that the she could enter the apartment. Melissa locked the door and the three of them stood awkwardly shifting from foot to foot.

"I'm Olivia. Why don't we sit?" She indicated the sofas.

"Kayla," the blonde said, and sat down on the sofa across from Olivia and Melissa.

"Why were you hiding when we opened the door?" Melissa asked.

"I wasn't. I started down the stairs because you didn't answer. As I was going down, I heard you open the door so I came back up."

Olivia looked the young woman over. She couldn't imagine why this girl had come to speak with them.

"How did you know the guys?" Melissa asked.

"I really only knew Christian. I work as a barista in a coffee shop in Kendall Square." Kayla clutched her hands together in her lap. "Christian would come in every day, sometimes twice a day. We'd talk. I'm a musician in a band. Christian came to see us play a few times. He invited me to the party that night."

"Do you generally wear a ski mask to parties?" Melissa asked.

Olivia flashed Melissa a look. She thought that getting information from Kayla would go better if their tone wasn't antagonistic.

"It was a Halloween party," Kayla said defensively. "Christian and I had been talking about Halloween and costumes. We were fooling about masks and knives." Her voice hitched. "I wore the mask to mess with him. As a joke."

"You were the one I saw in the hallway," Olivia said. Kayla nodded.

"What happened when you arrived at their place?" Olivia asked.

"I came up the back stairs. The back door was unlocked, I didn't have to buzz. I decided I'd put the mask on when I got to their door, knock, and scream when they opened it," Kayla said. "But the back door was open. They must have left it that way so they wouldn't have to keep answering the door when people arrived." She took a deep breath. "I put the ski mask on and went in. I walked down the hall. I heard someone using a blow dryer, but then ... I heard yelling. At first, I thought people were fooling around, but there was something, an edge to it that made it seem urgent, like they weren't kidding at all. I heard some knocking around, furniture moving or lamps falling. Thuds. I thought there must be a fight. I stayed where I was. Someone screamed. I was so scared, sort of frozen in place. A guy came out of the bathroom ... he didn't see me. He yelled something like, 'what's going on.' The hall was dark. He ran into the living room. I heard punches, a grunt, someone falling. I ducked into the room on my right, crouched down behind the bed and pressed against the floor. I heard running footsteps. I cursed myself for not rushing out the back as soon as I heard things going wrong."

Olivia watched Kayla's face closely. "Why didn't you just take off out the back way instead of going into the bedroom?"

"I had no time. If I ran for the back door, whoever was coming out of the living room would have seen me."

"What happened then?" Olivia asked.

"I could hear someone walking down the hall. He stopped at the room across from the one I was in... turned the doorknob...opened the door. The door to the room I was in was open already. I didn't shut it when I ran in there to hide. I could see his feet from under the bed. I could see his feet in the hall. I knew he was going to kill me." Beads of sweat had formed on Kayla's forehead. Her skin was ghostly pale. She leaned her head back on the sofa cushion.

"Did he come into the room you were in?"

Kayla shook her head. "No. You two came into the apartment just then. The guy took off out the back when he heard your voices."

Melissa and Olivia exchanged a long look realizing how close they'd come to being face to face with the killer.

"It was one guy?" Olivia asked.

"That's all I saw, but I can't be sure." Kayla leaned forward, putting her elbows on her knees and her head in her hands. "I didn't see anything that went on. I only heard it."

"Have you gone to the police?" Melissa asked.

"No." Her voice was small.

"Why did you run when I came down the hall?" Olivia asked, her blue eyes questioning.

Kayla looked up. "I just wanted out of there. I didn't know who was who or what was what. I panicked. All I wanted to do was escape."

"You should tell the police," Olivia said. "Tell them what you saw, and heard."

Kayla let out a long breath of air. "It wouldn't help. I only saw feet."

"It could help. When the police question you, something might come up that you forgot...or you suppressed," Olivia said.

"I don't think so." Kayla shifted on the sofa and put a hand up to her eyes.

No one said anything for a few moments, then Olivia thought of something and straightened up. "Did you follow me home the other night?"

Kayla blinked and hesitated. She looked like she wanted to stand up and dart from the apartment, but then she said, "Yes."

"Oh, thank heavens," Melissa said. "So it was you tailing Liv."

"I followed you," Kayla said, locking eyes with Olivia. "But I wasn't the only one who did."

9

An icy chill rippled down Olivia's back.

"What do you mean?" Melissa's voice sounded near a shriek. "Someone else was following Liv?"

Kayla ignored Melissa and said to Olivia, "I wanted to talk to you. To tell you I was in Christian's apartment the night of the murders. It wasn't hard to figure out what university you went to. I hung around campus looking for you. I happened to see you go into the library on Saturday. You were in there for hours."

"So you waited until I came out and followed me home?" Olivia asked.

"Yeah. It isn't very hard to do. I used to be a dancer. I know how to move, to be light on my feet. I kept you in my sights. I was quite a way back. I wasn't sure if I could talk to you that night, but I wanted to find out where you lived."

"Who else was following me?" Olivia braced for the answer.

"A young guy. Maybe a college student or someone trying to look like one. Average build, on the trim side. He had on dark corduroys, a dark wool jacket, cut like a baseball style jacket. He was wearing a baseball hat, was carrying a backpack."

"How do you know he was following me?"

"He was sitting outside the library for a long time. Then he went in and didn't come out until just after you left the building. He made every turn you did. I followed him, following you. When you stopped to tie your shoe, he stepped into the front yard of a house so you wouldn't see him."

"You saw all this?" Olivia's jaw was set. She couldn't believe that two people followed her home.

"Yeah. Like I said, it isn't hard to tail someone."

"What did he do when I got home?"

"That little park across from your building? It's more like a little common. He ducked in there. Sat on a bench for a while pretending to be texting, but he was watching your windows."

"Where were you when he was in the park?"

"I slipped two streets over, walked behind a few houses, came around behind him. I watched him for a while, and then I left."

"How long did he sit there? How long did you stay?" Olivia asked.

"An hour? But he was still there when I left."

"An hour?" Melissa's voice was high-pitched. She let out a curse. "Why didn't you call the police?"

"And say what?" Kayla's eyes flashed with annoyance. "I'd like to report a guy sitting on a bench, occasionally he glances at a building. I'm sure they would have rushed right over."

"Unfortunately, it's not against the law to sit in the park," Olivia said. "What color hair did he have?'

Kayla shrugged. "It was dark out. He had on the hat. Brown?"

"Long hair?"

"No. Not really short either. Cut like a regular guy's hair."

"That's not very specific," Melissa said.

"It's more than what you knew." Kayla's eyes bored into Melissa and then she turned to Olivia. "Watch your back. Who knows what he's up to, maybe nothing. But he was watching you."

"Thanks." Olivia's mind was racing. *Who the heck was following me? And, for what reason?*

"Do you think it's the killer who followed you?" Melissa asked. She looked frightened of the answer.

Olivia's eyes were wide. "How would he know who I was?"

Melissa gestured towards Kayla. "Well, *she* found out who you are."

"But the killer didn't see us at the apartment the night of the murders," Olivia said. "The killer was gone when we got there. How would he know who I was?"

"If he reads the paper, he knows who we are now, since that stupid newspaper printed our names," Melissa said.

"But I got followed the night before our names were in the paper."

"I don't know, Liv." Melissa shook her head. "Who knows who it was?"

"It could be harmless," Olivia said. "Maybe he's a reporter ... or maybe he's a guy worried about his safety and wanted to ask me about what I saw that night. Or it could have nothing to do with the murders at all."

"Well, that isn't comforting," Melissa groaned.

"It's possible that it was just someone looking for information ... and then he decided not to approach me," Olivia said.

Melissa made a disbelieving face, but said, "I hope so. I hope that's what it was."

Olivia turned to Kayla and asked, "Do you have any idea who would want to hurt Christian? Did he seem worried about anything? Had he ever been threatened?"

"He never told me anything like that," Kayla said.

"Never mentioned a fight with someone?" Olivia asked. "Or some trouble that his roommates were having with anybody? What about Gary? Did Christian ever say that Gary was having trouble with someone?"

"No, nothing," Kayla said. "Nothing like that came up. He wasn't worried about anything. At least, he never told me that he was."

A thought popped into Olivia's head. She hesitated, but then asked, "Were you and Christian together?"

A slight blush tinged Kayla's cheeks. "We hooked up a couple of times. It was casual."

"Can you think of anything else that might help? Anything that could point to someone who might have done this?"

Kayla shook her head. "I just wanted you to know that I wasn't the killer ... and, that you had a shadow following you around."

Olivia let out a long breath and nodded. "Thanks."

"I guess I'll take off then." Kayla rose from the sofa.

"Do you live around here?" Olivia asked.

"In Cambridge."

"Where do you work in Kendall? In case something comes up," Olivia said.

"Cream and Roses Café. It's right on Mass Ave."

"Let us know if you think of anything?" Olivia asked.

"Sure." Kayla started to move to the door as Olivia and Melissa stood up.

"Oh." Olivia bent towards the coffee table. "This is yours." She held the ski mask out to Kayla.

Kayla looked at the mask like she wanted nothing to do with it. "Where did you find that?"

"Right where you put it," Melissa growled.

Kayla looked blank. "I didn't put it anywhere. I ripped it off when I ran from Christian's apartment."

"Did you hang it from our doorknob?" Olivia asked.

"What? No." Kayla looked from Melissa to Olivia like they were crazy. "I threw it on the street."

"You haven't had it since the night of the murders?" Olivia asked.

Kayla shook her head. "No. I threw it down when I left Christian's apartment building."

"Where did you throw it?"

"I pulled it off after I ran from the apartment. I threw it as I ran. Maybe a few houses away from Christian's."

"Well, who the heck put it on our doorknob then?" Melissa asked.

"How would I know? I don't want it." Kayla pushed it back to Olivia. "Throw it away. I don't ever want to see it again."

"That makes two of us," Melissa said.

They walked Kayla to the door and Melissa locked

it after the young woman went out. Melissa watched through the peephole to be sure Kayla went down the stairs, and then she turned around and went back to her seat on the couch.

"What do you think?" Melissa asked.

"About what part?" Olivia plopped on the sofa and tossed the ski mask back on the coffee table.

"I don't know." Melissa rubbed at her temples.

Neither one spoke for a few minutes.

"How'd Kayla get into this building anyway?" Olivia asked.

"She must have buzzed some other apartment and they let her in."

"Great security," Olivia said. "What about the ski mask?"

"Do you believe she didn't hang it on our doorknob?" Melissa asked.

"She looked shocked when we told her it was on our doorknob. Either she didn't do it or she's a great actress."

"Who did it then?" Melissa's hands fiddled with the blanket draped over the arm of the sofa. "Did the killer do it?"

A cold chill ran over Olivia's shoulders. She didn't want to think that was a possibility so she brushed the idea away. "Is it someone playing a joke on us? Could that be all it is? Maybe it was someone who read about us being at the murder scene?"

"It isn't funny," Melissa said. Her face scrunched with anger.

Olivia changed the subject not wanting to think that the killer had been outside their apartment. "Did you notice Kayla blush when I asked if she and Christian were together?"

"I noticed she seemed a little uncomfortable."

"I'd bet it wasn't casual," Olivia said. "Why do I think there's more to what she told us?"

"About being with Christian?"

"That, yes, but what about other stuff too? Do you think she was telling the truth about a guy following me?"

A serious expression washed over Melissa's face. "I hadn't thought about that. Was it a lie?"

"It crossed my mind." Olivia stood up and moved to the window where she pushed the blind back an inch to look outside. "Did she say her last name?"

"I don't think so. I don't remember if she did."

Olivia spun towards Melissa. "Kayla was outside Jack's building when we were there, right after Jack was killed. How did she know that something happened to somebody? Why was she there? She said she lives in Cambridge. She isn't a student at this university. She wouldn't have gotten a tweet or a text about it."

Melissa leaned forward, wide-eyed, her mouth hanging open.

"I guess tweets could have spread out from the university community," Olivia said. "Maybe she knew Jack or has a friend who knew Jack? We should have asked her."

"It's possible," Melissa said. "She was there pretty darned fast though."

"Could she be the killer?" Olivia asked. "Could she be the one who killed all three of the guys? Did she just show up here to throw us off?"

Melissa's face blanched.

Olivia said, "Maybe we should wander down to Kendall Square someday and see if she really works at that café ... and ask her how she happened to be outside Jack's building right after he was killed."

Melissa narrowed her eyes. "*That* is a very good idea."

10

Olivia and Melissa trudged up the hill through campus heading to their morning classes.

"My back hurts." Melissa adjusted her backpack so that she could knead the muscles in her lower back with her fingers.

"Why don't I take the sleeping bag tonight and sleep on the floor in your room? Then you can sleep in your bed," Olivia told her. Melissa had been sleeping on the floor next to Olivia's bed since the night that Gary and Christian were killed.

"We could move my mattress into your room and put it on the floor," Melissa said.

"We're acting like babies," Olivia said.

Melissa sighed. "You're right. Like we said the other

night, the killer doesn't seem to be after women. He is only killing men so far. Maybe we're safe?"

Olivia said, "It seems like it." They were almost to their classroom buildings. "What about Kayla? Do you believe her story or not?" The friends had been discussing Kayla's visit off and on throughout the night and into the morning."

"I don't know. It's pretty odd that she happened to be at Christian and Gary's the night they were killed and was right outside Jack's building a little while after he was murdered. It makes me suspicious of her," Melissa said.

"I guess people could be suspicious of us, too, since we were at Christian's and Gary's the night they were killed and we spoke to Jack just before he was murdered. And we stood outside his building right after his body was found. We seem to be in odd places at odd times," Olivia said.

Melissa harrumphed.

"Meaning what?" Olivia asked.

"Meaning we're innocent. We have nothing to do with these killings."

"We just happen to be nearby when they happen," Olivia said.

"Correct."

"Using that logic, then Kayla is also innocent of any wrongdoing."

"If you had to guess," Melissa said, "what does your gut tell you about Kayla?"

"It tells me I need more information before I believe what she says, or not. We need to go to that café where she works and talk to her again."

"Yeah, and we ought to find the guy Christian was going to move in with," Melissa said. "Maybe he knows someone who had it in for Christian."

"We should try and contact him soon. It was Luke. What's his last name again?"

"Colleen said it was Smithson," Melissa said.

"That's it. She said he's at MIT. Let's look him up tonight, send him an email, ask to meet. Maybe he has some insight into why the guys were killed."

They approached the split in the walkway with one side heading to the science and engineering departments and the other leading to the humanities building.

"Are you going to be home for dinner?" Melissa asked.

"Yes. Why don't we cook something tonight?"

"Okay. Whatever you want to make is fine. I won't be back until 6pm. I have a lab this afternoon. If you want to wait for me, we can make dinner together."

WHEN MELISSA ARRIVED home after a long day of classes and lab, Olivia sat hunched over the coffee table intent on the papers in front of her. The room was warm and cozy with the lamplight casting a pleasant glow.

"What smells good in here?" Melissa asked as she put her backpack on the floor next to the sofa.

"I made veggie lasagna. I got back early. If you'd rather have something else, I can freeze it and we can eat it another time," Olivia said without looking up.

Melissa kicked off her shoes. "I don't want anything else. It smells delicious. Thanks for making it." She plopped next to Olivia. "I'm exhausted. Are you studying?"

"No. Look at this. I'm writing down facts about what has been happening."

Olivia had index cards laid out on the table in front of her. Each card had one fact with details written on it.

Melissa eyed the cards. She picked one up. It had "Christian" written at the top with details about him printed beneath his name. There was a card for each murder victim and cards for each person who was present at the apartment before the police were called. Olivia had a pad of paper in her lap and was writing a list of questions.

"I'm looking for patterns or connections that tie people together," Olivia said. "Like where they grew up, where they attended university, hobbies, clubs, friends. Things that might make them a target."

"Find anything?"

"Not really. Just that the guys who have been killed are recent graduates who had new jobs. They didn't go to the same university. They weren't all best friends. They weren't in the same field. They didn't have the same hobbies. Christian and Gary grew up in the same town and went through school together, but that doesn't link them to Jack."

"Maybe Jack only got killed because he happened to be at the apartment the night of the party?"

"I wondered about that," Olivia said. "I haven't been able to determine any real links between him and the other guys except that they were friends."

"Liv, do you think Kayla killed them?" Melissa pulled her legs up under her.

Olivia leaned back on the sofa, closed her eyes, and rubbed her forehead. "I don't know. Her story about being in the apartment was plausible. How could Kayla kill both guys all on her own? She doesn't look that strong." Olivia's eyes flicked open. "Is *one* person the link? Like all the guys knew Christian, so are all young men who knew Christian at risk?"

Melissa thought about that as she read over the cards on the table. "I don't know. That seems too vague. I keep going back to Kayla. If she had a knife and was fast, couldn't she kill two guys within seconds? She would have had surprise on her side."

"I guess she could have done it, but I'm having a hard time picturing her as the killer," Olivia said tapping the pen against her chin. "It's unusual that only men are the targets. Maybe we should look up serial killers and how they choose their victims and see if that helps us figure out what's going on here."

"Serial killer?" Melissa said. "This is a serial killer?"

"We should look up Luke Smithson after we eat and try to send him an email," Olivia said. "Ask him to meet with us to talk about Christian. See what he knows … see if he has any ideas."

"Yeah, good thinking. He should be easy to find on the MIT network. Maybe he can think of someone who had an argument or disagreement with Christian."

The oven timer went off and Olivia walked to the kitchen and pulled out the lasagna and a tray of garlic bread. She set them on top of the stove and the fragrant odor filled the apartment.

"I'm drooling," Melissa called. She took the plates and silverware and set the small table that was pushed up against one wall of the living room.

Olivia removed a salad from the refrigerator, carried it into the living room, and placed it on the table. "Maybe we should give this a rest. Stop thinking about it all the time and just let the cops figure it out. We don't have any idea how to solve a crime."

"It's just hard to stop thinking about it since we're the ones who found the bodies," Melissa said. "The image of the guys dead in their living room pops into my head off and on all day. It's horrible, Liv. I hate it. I wish it never happened."

"I know," Olivia said. "The same thing happens to me. It's in the back of my mind all day. I wake up at night in a cold sweat. That's why I've been trying to make some sense of it. It makes me feel less helpless."

Melissa gave a slight nod. She had dark circles under her brown eyes.

Olivia hated to see the sad look on her friend's face and wanted to make Melissa feel better, so she crossed to the coffee table and scooped up the index cards. "Let's take a break from thinking about it, for tonight anyway." She opened the drawer of the side table, plopped the index cards into it, and closed it. "There. Out of sight, out of mind."

"Good idea," Melissa said. "Let's just eat and talk about other things." She carried two dinner plates to the kitchen to get squares of lasagna and a piece of garlic bread for each of them. "Let's watch something mindless on television after dinner, maybe a crime show?" She caught herself and looked up at Olivia. They both smiled. "Um, so, maybe not a crime show."

Just as they sat down to dig in to their meals, the

intercom buzzed. The young women gave each other a look.

"Now what?" Melissa groaned.

Olivia got up, walked to their apartment door, and pushed the intercom button. "Who is it?"

A voice crackled over the speaker. "It's Luke Smithson. I was a friend of Christian."

Melissa stood up from the table, her eyes wide.

"Well, I guess we don't need to spend any time tracking him down tonight," Olivia told Melissa. She pressed the button to unlock the front door.

11

With Melissa standing right behind her, Olivia opened the door before Luke even reached the sixth floor landing.

"Thanks for letting me in. I'm Luke." He shook hands with the young women. "I wanted to talk to you." Luke had dark brown hair and golden brown eyes. He stood just under six feet tall, but because of his long legs, he gave the impression of being taller.

The girls introduced themselves.

"We're just sitting down to dinner. Why don't you join us? It's veggie lasagna. There's plenty," Olivia said. She gestured to the table.

"Oh, thanks. That'd be great. It smells really good." Luke removed his jacket and hung it over the side chair.

"We were planning on getting in touch with you," Melissa told him. "We were hoping to meet and talk."

Luke looked surprised. "Really?"

Olivia said, "We heard Christian was going to move in with you. We wanted to talk to you about him."

Melissa and Luke sat down at the table.

"How about some wine or a beer? There's soda, too ... or iced tea," Olivia said.

"A beer would be great."

Olivia went to the kitchen to get another plate, a napkin, and some silverware. She placed a square of lasagna and a slice of garlic bread on the plate, grabbed a beer from the fridge, and returned to the living room.

"We're sorry about Christian," Olivia told him as she set the food and beer on the table in front of him.

Luke shook his head. "It was a shock. No one expects a young person to pass away, let alone get murdered. At least, *I* never expected it." He coughed. Olivia could see tears welling in his eyes as he ate a few bites of the dinner. "The lasagna is really good." He put his fork down and took a long swig of beer. "I heard the two of you found him and Gary. Right after it happened?"

Melissa nodded.

"It was terrible," Olivia said. "When we saw them in the living room like that, my mind went blank, like my mind was separating from my body. I know that sounds strange, but the sight was so unexpected and horrible that my brain just turned off."

"I completely freaked out," Melissa said. "I was no help at all. I just shut down. Liv ran through the apartment trying to find Colleen."

"It was a stupid thing to do," Olivia said. "The killer could have been in the apartment. Like I said, I wasn't thinking clearly."

"It was a brave thing to do," Luke said.

"I'm sure you would have done the same," Olivia said.

Luke set his fork on his plate. He put his hands in his lap and looked down. "No, I wouldn't have." He shifted his gaze to the girls. "I didn't ... and I'm ashamed of myself."

Olivia and Melissa didn't say anything for several seconds wondering what the young man was talking about.

"What do you mean?" Melissa asked.

"I was there."

"At the apartment?" An icy shudder ran through Olivia. "Where? When?"

Luke took another long drink of his beer and let out a sigh. "I was at Christian's. The night they were killed. When I got there, Christian and Gary were in the living room. We talked for a minute. I brought beer. I went to the kitchen to put it in the fridge, and then I used the bathroom. While I was in there, I heard a shout. A scream. It chilled me. I knew it wasn't just the guys horsing around. I ran out of the bathroom, ran to the living room." Tears escaped from his eyes and he ran the back of his hand over his cheeks. "I ... I...."

Olivia reached over and held his arm. "It's okay. Don't tell us if it's too hard."

Luke swallowed. "Christian was in the chair. His throat. The blood. Gary was standing. The killer had his back to me, he grabbed Gary, he stabbed him. I shouted, I took a step into the room. The killer turned around." Luke ran his hands over his face. "He made a move towards me. He had the knife. He was going to kill me." A sob choked the young man for a few seconds. "Gary grabbed him from behind. The guy turned back to Gary and..." Luke stopped talking.

"What happened?" Olivia's voice was just above a whisper.

"I ran away."

The friends gaped at Luke.

"I ran away," Luke said in a hoarse whisper. "Just like a coward. If I stayed, if I tried to take the guy down, Gary might still be alive."

"If you stayed," Olivia said, still holding his arm, "you'd be dead too."

Luke lifted his wet eyes to Olivia. "I should have stayed."

Melissa brushed tears from her eyes.

"It's a natural reaction to protect ourselves. Self preservation is a powerful instinct," Olivia said.

"It was a natural reaction for *you* to go looking for Colleen," Luke said. "Not to run away."

"There wasn't a guy holding a knife standing two feet away from me," Olivia said.

"And I was good for nothing," Melissa told him. "Don't be hard on yourself. It would have been stupid for you to stay there."

Olivia leaned forward. "You saw the killer's face?"

Luke shook his head. "He was wearing a mask."

Olivia's posture deflated.

"He had on a black ski mask," Luke said.

"The ski mask. So, one of the people who left the apartment wearing a ski mask is definitely the killer." Olivia and Melissa looked pointedly at each other.

Luke nodded. "Wait. What do you mean 'one of the people'?"

Olivia said, "A witness saw two people wearing ski masks leave the apartment building that night. But they didn't leave together."

"Two people? But I only saw one killer."

"Did you go to the police?" Melissa asked. "Did you tell them what you saw?"

"Yeah. I went there that night. I tried to downplay my cowardice. I saw you two there at the police station. I overheard that you found the bodies."

"Why did you want to talk to us?" Melissa asked.

"Because, you were there. You found them. I wanted to know if you saw the killer, too. If you knew anything, anything at all."

Olivia's hands were sweaty and anxiety pulsed through her body. Talking about the night of the killings made her heartbeat speed up and her breathing become quick and shallow. *Poor Luke. It must be worse for him. I didn't even know the guys. Gary and Christian were his friends. He saw it happen.*

"You okay, Liv?" Melissa could see her own distress mirrored in Olivia's face.

"I'm okay. Talking about it … well, you know." Olivia gulped from her water glass. She held the cool surface of the glass against her temple for a few seconds and then she turned to Luke. "Do you know Kayla?"

"Who?"

"Kayla. She's a little taller than me, slim, has spikey blonde hair. She told us she had been hooking up with Christian."

Recognition flickered in Luke's eyes. "Oh, the girl from the coffee shop. I never met her. Christian talked about her sometimes. Why?"

"She was at Christian's apartment that night. She came in the back door. She heard the attack."

Luke's mouth opened in surprise. "She was there? When it was happening?"

Olivia nodded. "That's what she said. I saw her,

when I went down the hall to find Colleen. I didn't know at the time that it was Kayla. I thought it was the killer. She said she was hiding in the bedroom. She stepped out of the last bedroom ... she was dressed all in black, was wearing a ski mask as part of her costume. She saw me and took off."

"She was there? She was wearing a ski mask?" Luke asked. "She says she heard the murders?"

"Yeah," Melissa said.

"I didn't know," Luke said. "She must have come in when I was in the bathroom."

"Probably," Olivia said.

"She was wearing a ski mask?" Luke's forehead was wrinkled in puzzlement.

"I saw her," Olivia said.

"That's a weird coincidence," Luke said.

"Jack Wilson, a student at the university, said he saw two different people leave the building wearing ski masks. They left at different times. You saw the killer with a ski mask and Kayla was wearing one. So that confirms there were two people with ski masks at the apartment," Melissa said.

"Jeez." Luke ran his hand through his hair. "I was there. Kayla was there. Colleen was there. And still, Christian and Gary are dead. I don't know how I can live with this."

"You can't second guess," Olivia told him. "The killer had a knife. Maybe, other weapons. You three wouldn't stand a chance against an armed man. He had surprise on his side. You couldn't fight him bare-handed. There would just have been more dead bodies there."

"Why don't you see a counselor? Talk about it with someone," Melissa said. "It could help."

"Maybe," Luke said." It didn't seem like he would though.

"Colleen said Christian was moving in with you?" Olivia asked.

"Yeah. He had already brought some of his stuff over. We met at MIT. I'm a senior there."

"Did he ever mention an enemy? Somebody he had a fight with?"

"No. No one. He never talked about anything like that. He wasn't worried about anything. I suppose there could have been something, but he never said a word to me that anything was wrong."

"Do you think the attack on them was random?" Melissa asked.

Luke didn't hesitate. "No. I don't."

"Why not?" Olivia asked.

"I don't know." He shrugged. "Just the feeling I have."

"We thought we'd go to the coffee shop some day. Talk to Kayla again. See if she remembers anything else. You want to meet us there when we go?"

"Maybe. Yeah, okay. It might help to put our heads together," Luke said.

Olivia glanced at Luke's jacket hanging over the arm of the sofa and thought of something. She sat up straight. "Luke. Did you follow me home the other night?"

Luke's eyebrows went up in surprise, and then he looked sheepish. "Yeah, I did. You saw me?"

Olivia nodded. "You scared me to death."

"I'm sorry. I wanted to see where you lived. I wanted to talk to you. But I couldn't get up the nerve to ring your apartment."

"That's why you sat in the park across from the building?"

"You saw me there?"

"No, but Kayla did."

Luke's brow furrowed in confusion.

"Kayla was following me that night, too," Olivia said. "She was behind you. She saw you tailing me."

Luke shook his head. "I can't even tail someone right."

"Don't worry about it," Melissa said. "It's probably not a skill you'll ever need."

The corners of Olivia's mouth turned up at Melissa's comment. "You want another beer?" she asked Luke.

"Yes. Please," Luke said.

Olivia got up to go the kitchen, but pivoted

abruptly. She stared back at Luke. "Are you living alone?"

"Yeah."

Melissa's face turned white.

"Why do you ask?" Luke asked.

"You know Jack is dead?"

"Jack who?"

"Jack Wilson. He came into the apartment right after us on the night of the killings. He was the witness who saw the two people in ski masks leaving the building."

Luke look confused.

"Jack was stabbed to death," Olivia told him. "Just the other night."

"It seems the killer could be the same person who killed Gary and Christian," Melissa said.

An expression of horror washed over Luke's face. "Someone else was killed?"

"Didn't you hear the news?" Olivia asked.

"I went home for a few days, to Chicago. I didn't pay any attention to the news. I just got back a couple of hours ago."

"Luke," Olivia said. "Three guys who were at Christian's apartment that night are dead." She looked him square in the eyes. "You're the fourth guy who was there that night. The killer saw you."

Luke's eyes widened in understanding and the

blood drained out of his face. "Could you get me that beer now? I think I need it."

Olivia brought two beers and a glass of iced tea back to the living room. They moved to the couches and sat sipping their drinks.

"Maybe you should move in with a friend," Olivia suggested. "You shouldn't be alone."

"Who's going to want me to move in with them?" Luke asked. "Hey guys, mind if I move in? Oh, and don't mind that person with a knife following me around."

"You can move in here with us," Melissa said.

Olivia smiled at Melissa. She was proud of her friend for offering Luke a place to stay so he wouldn't be alone.

Luke looked surprised. "No. Thanks, but no. I'm not going to be driven out of my home and I'm certainly not going to put you two at risk. Wait. You were at Christian's. Why aren't you worried about your own safety?"

"Well, sometimes we are," Melissa said. She wasn't going to admit that she was sleeping on the floor next to Olivia's bed every night.

"It seems the killer is only after men," Olivia said. "So far, anyway."

"Only men?" Luke said. "But, why?"

"Who knows? Who knows anything about this

mess?" Melissa said. Her voice was weary with exhaustion.

"I don't know why either," Olivia said. "But there must be a way to find some shred of information that will answer 'who.'"

12

Olivia, Melissa, and Luke arranged to meet at the Kendall Square coffee shop where Kayla worked. Luke had a class and told them he would arrive later.

Olivia and Melissa opened the door and saw Kayla working behind the counter mixing coffee drinks. A young man was taking orders and the friends got in line. Kayla glanced their way and did a double-take. She nodded a greeting to them, but she looked a bit flustered.

The young man taking the orders was slim, average height, with short blonde hair, blue eyes, and a welcoming smile. He was so similar in coloring to Kayla that Olivia wondered if they were siblings. The guy chatted jovially with the customers and he even broke into song, singing several bars of a popular hit. The people in line loved it.

"Well, lovely ladies," he beamed at Olivia and Melissa. "What will it be?"

Oliva and Melissa gave him their orders and bantered back and forth with the amusing employee, then moved further down the counter to wait for their drinks. With a serious face, Kayla made eye contact as she snapped a cover on a completed order.

"Do you have time to chat?" Melissa asked her.

"I'm off in thirty minutes if you want to wait. Is something new?"

"No, we just want to talk ... put our heads together," Olivia said.

"Come sit with us when you're ready," Melissa told her.

The girls found an empty table in the crowded café and sat down. Melissa pulled out her iPad and Olivia used her phone to check messages.

After fifteen minutes, Luke came through the door, scanned the room, spotted the young women at the table, and headed over to sit with them.

"I just got out of class. It went overtime. I worried I might miss you."

"Kayla doesn't get off her shift for another ten minutes or so."

"Are there any updates? Have you heard anything new about the murders?" Luke asked.

"Nothing," Melissa said. "There hasn't been anything in the news. They just rehash what's already known."

"Which isn't much," Olivia said.

Kayla came from behind the counter. A flash of apprehension passed over her face when she saw Luke sitting with Melissa and Olivia. She stood awkwardly next to their table.

"Hey," Olivia said. "Come sit."

"Is everything okay?" Kayla asked in a small voice. She glanced at Luke.

"I'm Luke."

"Kayla," she told him, as she took a seat.

Olivia said, "Luke was in the apartment the night Christian and Gary got killed. He was in another room and heard the fight."

Kayla's eyes widened. Olivia couldn't tell if her expression was one of surprise or fear.

"I was there, too," Kayla whispered. Her eyes looked moist.

"They told me you were there," Luke said.

"I didn't see the killer. Just his feet. I was on the floor hiding behind the bed," Kayla told him.

Luke didn't want to share what he saw that night or that he'd run away. "I was a friend of Christian's."

"I know. I recognize you," Kayla told him. "I've seen you with Christian."

"We thought maybe, we could talk," Melissa said.

"See if we can come up with anything new since the four of us are connected to that night."

"Like what?" Kayla asked. She fidgeted with a napkin on the table.

"Maybe someone will remember something that seemed unimportant earlier," Olivia said. "Maybe we could go over what happened to each of us, tell about getting to the apartment, what happened when we arrived, when we left. Try to remember the little things that were going on around us."

Melissa said, "That's a good idea. Let me think back on the night. I'll start. I'll tell what I remember."

Melissa gave her impressions and then Olivia told what she recalled. Nothing seemed out of the ordinary. Nothing stood out as suspicious. Luke went next. He told about walking to the apartment, what he saw on the way, what happened when he arrived.

"I'm full of guilt," he said. "I'm struggling with why my friends are dead and I'm still alive. I wish I could go back in time and make it right."

The cheerful, blonde barista approached the table with a platter holding samples of banana bread and pumpkin bread. "Hey, guys. Free treats." He lowered the tray and offered the bread selections to the group. Nobody was hungry, so they declined the samples.

Kayla introduced him. "This is my friend, Eric."

Melissa, Olivia, and Luke greeted him.

"You're at MIT," Luke said. "Same department as me, right?"

"Yeah, I had a double major though, spent more time in electrical engineering. I graduated last May." Eric moved away with the platter to the next table.

Melissa asked, "You want to tell what happened, Kayla? Tell us what you saw that night?"

"I already told you," she snapped. She looked at the tabletop and then lifted her hands to cover her eyes.

Olivia and Melissa glanced at each other.

"I know you told us things already, but something new might come up if you think back on it again," Olivia said gently. "I know it's hard."

Kayla's head jerked up. "You don't know how hard it is." The rims of her eyelids were red. "I can't keep thinking about it and thinking about it. Let the police figure it out."

"You and Luke were the only ones in the apartment when it happened. Remembering something, any little thing, could shed important information on who did it," Melissa said. "It could help."

"Help what?" Kayla asked. "They're dead. They're not coming back. Why keep going over it? It's too late to help them." She pushed her chair back and stormed into the back room of the coffee shop. Her friend, Eric, followed after her.

Luke leaned forward. "Why can't she talk about it? I'm the one who should have the hardest time talking about it." He shook his head. "She didn't see it like I did. She didn't let them down like I did. She didn't find the bodies like you two did."

Melissa kept her voice low. "When she came to see us the other night, she said she didn't want people to think she was the killer. She didn't tell the police she was there. Why won't she talk to the police? What does she have to hide?"

"I'd like to ask her how she happened to be outside Jack Wilson's building right after he was killed," Olivia said. "How did she know what was going on? How did she happen to be in the neighborhood? She doesn't live anywhere near there."

Luke leaned forward. "You think she has something to do with these murders?"

"I'm not sure, I'm only speculating," Olivia said. "It's possible Kayla did it, but is it probable? It must just be coincidence that she was at both crime scenes, that she was wearing a ski mask like the killer. It's a coincidence, isn't it? I mean Melissa and I were at both crime scenes and we didn't kill them."

Kayla came out of the back room wearing her jacket with her bag slung over her shoulder. She headed for the exit and, with a hard expression, glanced at the three of them sitting at the table as she pushed the door open. Her friend Eric returned to work the counter.

"Guess we won't be talking to Kayla anymore today," Olivia said.

Melissa rolled her eyes. "Should we come back again another day?"

"I know Kayla plays with her band on Thursday nights at a club," Luke said. "Christian and I went to see them once, we only stayed for one set. That must be where she recognized me from. We could go there and see if she'd talk to us after they played."

"It couldn't hurt," Olivia said. "Unless, she has us thrown out of the club."

13

Olivia, Melissa, and Luke took seats at a table in the alternative rock club. The place was full and they were lucky to see people vacate some seats in time to grab them before others did. There was a small stage and Kayla's band was playing mid-set.

"They're good." Olivia had to raise her voice to be heard over the music.

Luke went to the bar and returned with drinks.

"I'm nervous," Melissa said. "What if she gets angry with us?"

Olivia shrugged. "Then she won't talk to us. We have every right to frequent this club. We're not causing any trouble."

"Uh oh," Luke said. "Look who's heading our way."

Kayla's friend, Eric, the barista, was walking

straight across the room to where they were sitting. He did not have a smile on his face.

"Here to hassle Kayla again?" Eric stood over them holding his drink.

"Why don't you sit with us?" Olivia asked. "We don't want to bother her. That isn't our aim."

"What is your aim then?" Eric took a seat.

"We're just trying to figure out what happened to our friends," Melissa told him. "If we all put our heads together, maybe we can come up with something that will lead to the killer."

"Isn't that law enforcement's job?" Eric took a swig from his glass.

"Melissa and I found the bodies," Olivia said. "We want to do something to help. Maybe something small could help solve it."

"And, what about you?" Eric directed his question to Luke. "Did you find the bodies, too?"

"I was there," was all Luke would say.

The band stopped playing and the performers left the stage for a break. Recorded music blared from the club's speakers and people stood up and milled around talking while some headed to the bar.

"Do you think Kayla would talk to us?" Melissa asked Eric.

"I don't know. What do you want to ask her? What do you think she knows?" Eric held his glass up and swirled the liquid around in it.

Olivia said, "We just want to get her impressions from the night. Or, maybe she could tell us something about Christian that might help."

"Like what? That he was a dirt bag?" Eric asked.

"Why the hell would you say that?" Luke's eyes narrowed in anger.

"Because, he dumped her. He used her, and then threw her away like she was trash."

"Eric." Everyone at the table turned towards the voice. Kayla stood two feet away from them, her face pinched with embarrassment.

Eric reached for her hand and spoke to her softly. "I'm sorry, Kayla, but it's true. He was no good."

Kayla sat down in the empty seat. She looked each of the people in the eyes, and then shifted her gaze down. "Christian broke off with me, a few days before the party. I wasn't invited to their Halloween party. I decided to go anyway, to try to talk to him. But, you know how that worked out."

"You wanted to try to get back together?" Melissa asked.

"I don't know why on earth you wanted that," Eric said, exasperated.

Kayla's eyes filled with tears. "Because ... I loved him."

Awkward silence fell over the group.

"I'm sorry," Olivia said. She touched Kayla's shoulder.

"He didn't care about you, Kayla. You were a hookup. That was all," Eric said. "You wouldn't see it. He thought he was better than you."

"Christian wasn't like that," Luke said with force in his tone.

"Oh, come on." Eric faced Luke. "He was an entitled rich boy."

"Did you know him?" Melissa asked.

Eric flashed his eyes at Melissa, his jaw muscles tense. "I met him once. That was enough. It wasn't hard to see what he was."

"That seems unfair," Olivia said. "You can't judge someone from one meeting."

"Can I judge someone by how they treat my friend?" Eric glared at Olivia.

"Eric," Kayla said softly. She picked at the sleeve of her sweater.

"Kayla, you were blind to it. You let him use you. You made more of it than it was because you fell for a rich, pretty boy's charms."

"You're just projecting your own stereotypical ideas onto Christian," Luke said.

"He hurt her. Seems like he fit the stereotype."

"Maybe you should mind your own business." Luke shoved his chair back and stood. He scowled at Eric, opened his mouth to speak, but changed his mind and stomped away to the bar.

"You didn't know Christian," Kayla told Eric. "He was a good guy."

Eric rolled his eyes. "He was not. Anyway, I don't care about him. I care about you."

The band members started to return to the stage and Kayla rose from her seat to go take her place with them. Eric held her hand for a moment and gave it a squeeze before she moved away to the stage.

"How did you and Kayla meet?" Olivia asked, trying to ease the tension around the table.

Eric shifted in his seat and lifted his glass. "We met at the coffee shop. We've been working there for a couple of years. I started there my senior year of college."

"You said you went to MIT?" Melissa asked.

"Yeah. I double majored, computer science and electrical engineering."

"Are you looking for work in your field?" Melissa questioned.

"I was working, at a start-up. I got laid off. So it was back to the coffee shop for me."

"We have some friends working at start-ups. What company was it?" Olivia asked. "Something in Kendall?" Many of the Cambridge area start-up companies were located in the Kendall Square area.

"It was LearnApp." Eric took the last swallow of his drink and placed the glass on the table with a thud. "Educational products. It wasn't for me."

"Well, I'm sure you'll find something else soon," Olivia said.

"I'm in no rush. I'm working on a project of my own, and I enjoy the coffee shop. For, now." Eric fiddled with the empty glass then lifted his eyes to Olivia and Melissa. "You should leave Kayla alone. Don't draw her into this."

Melissa said, "She's already involved in it."

"We're all upset by the killings," Olivia said. "We can't just forget what we saw. It's important to talk about it. Look for clues. Maybe there's something we saw that could help identify the killer."

"Why won't Kayla tell the police she was there that night? She says she loved Christian. Why won't she help?" Melissa asked.

Eric's face took on a sour expression as he turned to Melissa. "Kayla and the police don't get along."

"What do you mean?" Olivia asked.

"Kayla had a run in with the cops a couple of years ago. She has a record. For assault."

The girls' eyes went wide.

"Assault?" Melissa's voice cracked.

"She had an abusive boyfriend, but she was the one who ended up arrested," Eric said. He ran his finger around the rim of his empty glass. "So she's not too keen on sharing information with the cops." Eric stood up. "I'm heading to the bar. I'll see you."

After a few minutes, Luke came back to the table and took a seat. "Where'd the rude weasel go?"

"To the bar," Melissa said. "Listen to this." Melissa told Luke about Kayla having a police record.

"Now I understand why she wouldn't want to tell the police she was at Christian's the night he was killed," Olivia said.

"If she was arrested for assault once ... maybe ... maybe Kayla killed them." Melissa's face was white.

"Eric said Kayla's boyfriend was abusive. The assault could have been self defense," Olivia said. She didn't want to believe that Kayla was capable of killing someone. "How could Kayla kill them? She couldn't kill two guys. Could she?"

Nobody knew what to say to that.

"It wasn't Eric's place to tell people that Kayla has a record," Luke said.

"Eric has strong opinions. He wants us to leave Kayla alone," Olivia said. She glanced towards the bar. "And he is definitely into Kayla."

"Is he?" Luke asked. "I thought he was gay."

Melissa smiled. "Jeez, Luke, really? He is so not gay."

"I don't see Kayla with *him*," Luke said. "Ever. He's like some old, cranky neighbor with his nose in all your business. What would she see in him? He's nuts if he thinks she'd ever be with him."

"I think he's just watching out for his friend,"

Melissa said. "Nobody wants to see a friend get hurt."
As soon as the words were out of her mouth, she
wished she hadn't said them.

"Exactly," Luke said. "Seeing friends get hurt is...."
Sadness and guilt pulled at him.

"Why don't we get out of here," Olivia said. "We
aren't going to be able to ask Kayla anything more
tonight and I'm not in the mood for a place like this.
It's too crowded, too loud."

"Good idea," Melissa said. "Let's go."

The three vacated the table and walked into the
cool night air, chatting as they strolled to the subway.

"So Kayla wasn't even supposed to be at the party.
She wasn't invited," Olivia said. "She decided she
would just show up so she could see Christian."

"She wanted to talk to Christian about getting back
together," Melissa said.

"I wonder how angry she was when he dumped
her." Olivia raised her eyebrows in a questioning look.

"Do you think she was angry enough to do something violent?" Luke asked.

"We still don't know how she was outside Jack's
building right after he was murdered," Melissa said.

"If Kayla is the killer, what could have been her
motive for killing Jack?" Olivia asked. "She could have
killed Christian because he broke off with her and
Gary was just in the way. But why kill Jack?"

Luke said, "Jack saw her. She might have eliminated him because he saw her leave the apartment. She could have been afraid that he was actually able to identify her."

Melissa said, "Could she have been with the killer? They both had on ski masks. Were they working together? Are there two killers?"

Even though Olivia really couldn't picture Kayla as a killer, the possibility chilled her. Her mind was a tangled mass of bits and pieces of information that didn't seem to lead anywhere.

Melissa's voice shook. "We saw Kayla in the apartment. If she *is* a killer, does that mean we're all in danger?"

That same question had been worrying Olivia's mind for days.

14

Olivia was standing under a streetlight on the sidewalk outside of the university engineering building when Ynes drove up. They decided to take Ynes' car since she drove a black Honda CRV which was less conspicuous than Olivia's orange Jeep and it would be better for their clandestine mission. As soon as Olivia sat down in the passenger seat and closed the door, Ynes hit the gas pedal hard causing Olivia's head to jerk back.

"Sorry," Ynes said looking over her left shoulder at the oncoming traffic. "I'm jittery."

"You okay to drive?" Olivia snapped her seatbelt into place as Ynes careened into traffic.

"I'd be more nervous if I was just sitting in the car *not* driving. It gives me something to focus on."

"We're just going to the gym to find out about

membership, remember?" Olivia said. "That's all it has to be. No one knows any different. That's our story if anyone sees us."

Ynes flashed Olivia a look. "Yeah, right."

They drove along the roads out of Somerville not speaking for a few minutes, and then Olivia said, "Melissa is going to park a few buildings up from the gym near the end of the street. The road's a dead end. There won't be many cars going to the end of the road at this time of night so fewer people will see Melissa parked there. She'll wait for our text saying everything went okay. If she doesn't hear from us in the agreed upon amount of time, she'll drive over and if she doesn't see us, she'll call the police."

"Do you think Adam Johnson will show up while we're in the gym looking at his locker?" Ynes' hands were shaking on the wheel. "Eva says he just shows up anytime. Unexpectedly. Acts like he owns the place."

"Are you sure you can do this?" Ynes' jittery behavior was making Olivia nervous.

"I'm going to do it," Ynes said. "You're not going in there alone. Eva's my friend. I'll be okay once we get there."

Watching Ynes' nervous movements while she sat in the driver's seat maneuvering the car along the dark streets, Olivia wasn't so sure that Ynes would be able to pull this off. She worried what might happen if Adam Johnson or someone else caught them at the gym.

"There's nothing to be nervous about." Olivia tried to reassure Ynes. "We're potential clients. That's all. If the coast is clear, we'll investigate. If it doesn't seem safe, we'll call it off. We won't do anything stupid."

Ynes blew out a long breath. "Yes. Right. You're right."

They traveled out of the neighborhoods and entered an industrial area with large concrete buildings and large parking lots lining both sides of the road. The lots were mostly empty, some had a car or two scattered here and there. Security lamps high on the buildings pointed beams of light near the buildings' entrances, leaving most of the areas in shadow.

"Why does this gym have to be in such a desolate area?" Ynes moaned.

"The gym should be the next building on the left. There. There it is." Olivia pointed and Ynes guided the car into the dark parking area.

The gym was closed and there was only one small vehicle parked close to the front door. Ynes pulled next to it, she and Olivia got out of the car, and they walked to the parked vehicle.

The window slid down. An attractive dark haired woman with caramel-colored skin and dark eyes sat behind the wheel. She reached her hand out to Ynes.

"Here are the keys. They're spares. One's for the gym door, the other is for Adam Johnson's locker. Put everything in the locker back the way you found it. Go in the back way." Her eyes kept flicking up to look in the rear view mirror, checking to be sure no one was around. "Try not to be inside too long. Don't turn on the lights."

Ynes took the keys and gestured to Olivia. "This is my friend..."

The woman in the car cut her off. "Don't introduce us. I don't want to know her name. The less I know the better. I'm getting out of here now. Don't stay inside long. Be careful. Good luck." She started her car, backed away, and pulled out of the lot and into the street.

"So obviously that was Eva," Olivia said.

"Yes." Ynes watched the taillights of Eva's car disappear down the street. "I've never seen her so nervous." She faced Olivia. "Do you think we should do this? Maybe it's a bad idea."

"You thought it was a good idea when we planned it," Olivia said gently. "It'll be okay. If something goes wrong, we have our story rehearsed. We practiced it. We'll be all right." She took Ynes' elbow and steered her to the back of the building. "I wish we could get your car out of sight, but there isn't anyplace to put it that we could get to it fast. It's like a concrete desert around here. We'll just have to be quick."

A cold breeze stirred up some sand from the lot and blew it against their faces. "Ugh." Ynes blinked the dirt from her eyes. "From bad to worse."

They moved to the rear of the building and found the back door. There was a dumpster placed beside it.

"Here. Take the keys. My hands are shaking too much," Ynes said.

Olivia took them and inserted one in the lock. "I hope there isn't a security alarm that Eva forgot to tell us about." Turning the key, she gave the heavy metal door a tug. "It's open. Come on." Olivia reached into her pocket for her penlight and switched it on.

They entered a dark, back room with some trash receptacles scattered around, a few cardboard boxes tossed to the side, and several large replacement containers of water for a cooler. A hallway led off the room.

The girls followed along the corridor, Olivia leading the way and Ynes behind her clutching Olivia's jacket. Olivia flashed the small beam of the penlight along the floor and walls. There were a couple of office doors along the hallway. The corridor ended and opened into a huge workout room filled with weights and exercise machines.

A reception desk stood close to the gym's front door. Some light from the outside security lamps filtered in through the big plate glass windows at the front of the room making it a little easier to see. Gym equipment stood throughout the room like silent creatures cloaked in shadow waiting to pounce.

"I don't like it in here," Ynes whispered.

"The locker rooms must be over that way." Olivia used the penlight beam to point across the room to the far wall. They shuffled to the other side of the area being careful not to trip over the free weights strewn about and entered the space that had the 'Men's Locker Room' sign over the door jamb. Lockers lined three of the room's walls. A shower section was off to one side and a small room with urinals, stalls and sinks was to the left.

"It smells in here." Ynes scrunched up her nose.

"Which locker belongs to Adam Johnson?" Olivia ran the tiny beam over the row of lockers.

Ynes didn't speak. Her face was blank.

"Ynes?" Olivia whispered.

"Oh, hell. Eva didn't tell me," Ynes said. "I forgot to ask for specifics. I thought the locker number would be on the key."

"Good idea. Let's see." Olivia fished the keys from her pocket. She lifted the penlight and pointed the beam as she and Ynes hunched over and looked at the one in Olivia's palm.

"Nothing," Ynes moaned. "How can we figure it out?"

"I wonder if there's a master list of locker assignments at the reception desk," Olivia said. "Go look and I'll search around in here. Maybe there's a list on one of these walls. Take the penlight. Don't fall and break an ankle."

Ynes took the light and moved into the darkness of the workout room. Olivia, straining to see in the shadowy space, crept around the locker room looking for a list taped to one of the walls.

After a few minutes passed, Olivia heard Ynes, breathing hard, hurry back into the room, and when she turned to her, the penlight beam held in Ynes' hand caught Olivia directly in the eyes.

"Ynes." Olivia snapped her eyes shut and simultaneously raised her hand to shield her face.

Ynes shifted the beam away from Olivia.

"Did you find the list?" Olivia asked.

Ynes quickly sidled up next to Olivia and whispered, her voice strained. "Two cars just parked near the front door. I saw two guys get out. I think they're coming in."

15

The girls stood frozen in place for several seconds, until Olivia rushed to the locker room door that led into the workout room and carefully closed it trying not to make a sound. They heard the front doorknob clunking and men's voices speaking. Olivia grabbed Ynes by the arm and hurried her across the room to the bathrooms.

"We're trapped in here." Ynes' voice quavered.

Olivia opened the door of a small storage closet, shoved Ynes inside, stepped in, and clicked the door shut. Her heart hammered. She tried to slow her breathing. Ynes was holding so tightly to Olivia's arm that she was afraid the blood supply to her hand would be cut off. Heavy footsteps crossed the workout room and moved into the locker area.

"It's in here," a deep voice said. "Where's the damn light switch?"

Light filtered through the space at the bottom of the closet door and Olivia prayed that their feet couldn't be seen from the other side.

Ynes leaned close to Olivia. Olivia raised her index finger to her lips urging Ynes not to make a sound.

"How do you have a key to this place anyway?" The voice seemed to belong to a smaller or, at least, a less hefty man.

"I know the owner," the deeper voice said.

The young women could hear the metallic clank of a locker door being flung open.

"Here it is." A zipper moved over what sounded like a gym bag or a backpack. "Here. Try it."

They heard rustling, a sniffing sound, and then coughing.

"Good stuff. Oh, yeah."

"Let's have the cash," the husky voice said.

Ynes squeezed Olivia's arm. A drug deal was going down between the two guys and they understood what would happen to them if they were discovered in their hiding spot. Standing like statues, they kept their breathing soft and shallow.

Ynes closed her eyes and started to silently pray. Olivia's hands were wet with sweat and her heart was thudding so hard she was afraid the men would be able to hear its hammering beat.

"It's right here, don't worry. I always pay." More rustling sounds could be heard. "Whose car is outside anyway?"

"I told you," the deeper voice said. "Some client's car must have broken down. Relax. Do you see anyone around? We're alone."

"Look, Adam, you can't be too careful," the smaller man said. "I got interests to look out for."

The bigger man snorted. "Yeah, the only interests you need to look out for are your own."

"That's right. It's a tough world. I don't play football like you do, so I got to make my own way."

Oh, no, Olivia thought. *It's Adam Johnson doing this deal.* The girls could hear things being shoved into a bag. The locker slammed shut. Footsteps moved away. The light flicked off. The men left the locker room and moved through the workout area. Their voices could be heard, but the words were hard to make out. The front door of the gym opened and then slammed closed.

Olivia and Ynes let out long breaths and slumped against the storage closet's walls.

"That was close." Ynes voice was soft and shaky and she sounded like she was near tears.

"Let's give them a minute and then we'll slip out the back door where we came in," Olivia said close to Ynes' ear. "If they knew we heard what just happened..." She shuddered and didn't finish the thought. Her lower back ached from holding herself so tensely. All she wanted was to get the heck out of the building and run to their car.

After a few minutes, Ynes said, "How about now? You think we can go now?"

Olivia asked, "I'm pretty sure which bank of lockers they were standing near. You want to try and open them and look at what Johnson has in there?"

"I think we should get out of here. What if he comes back?" Ynes' voice trembled.

"Okay. It's just that we're in here already. Should we take the chance and try to figure out which locker is Johnson's?"

"I vote no," Ynes said. "I want to get out of here."

"Okay. Let's step out of the closet and listen. Keep the penlight off." Olivia slowly turned the knob of the supply closet door and eased it open. She stepped out and stopped, straining to hear. She gestured for Ynes to follow. They crept to the door that led into the workout room and slowly made their way through the space.

Unable to see the front parking lot from where they stood, neither of them could tell if the guys were outside or if they had driven away. Olivia and Ynes hugged the wall to stay in shadow and inched along to the hallway that led to the back door.

Once they turned into the corridor they quickened their pace, with Olivia in the lead, running her hand along the wall to help find her way in the dark. Ynes held to Olivia's jacket. When they reached the back door of the gym, Olivia halted and put her ear to the door, and hearing nothing, pulled hard to open it and stepped out into the cool night air. Ynes turned the lock and pushed against the door to shut it. They stood still listening for anything that might indicate that the men were nearby.

"Let's go to the corner and peak around into the parking lot to see if their cars are still there," Olivia suggested.

"Wait a sec," Ynes said. She leaned back against the side of the building with her eyes closed. Her chest was heaving.

"You okay?" Olivia asked.

"I just need to catch my breath. I almost fainted in there."

"Bend over a bit," Olivia told her. She placed her hand on Ynes' shoulder. "Or sit down and put your head between your knees."

Before Ynes could respond, a deep voice growled at them from the corner of the building. "What are you doing back there?"

Olivia's heart flew into her throat. She spun towards the voice to see Adam Johnson's dark form striding towards them. Her stomach lurched with fear.

"Who are you?" Johnson sneered. "What are you doing back here?" He towered over the women, his face showing a hard grimace in the beam of the rooftop security light.

Ynes slumped into a sitting position on the ground, pretending to be drunk like they had planned if someone caught them, but ready to spring up if Johnson laid a hand on Olivia.

"Who are *you*?" Olivia pretended she didn't know who the man was. Forcing her voice to sound angry, she stood protectively next to Ynes and then slipped her hand into her jacket pocket. She pushed the gym keys further down into the pocket and pulled out her phone. "Keep back. I'll call the cops. What do you want?"

Johnson moved closer to intimidate Olivia. "I asked you a question. What are you doing back here?" He smacked Olivia's hand causing the phone to fall with a clunk onto the concrete and clatter away. Johnson shoved Olivia and her back hit against the wall of the building. Ynes shifted her eyes to watch what was happening.

"What are you doing?" Olivia yelped. "Get away from us."

Ynes stayed in her slumped position, but moved her head slightly so that she could keep Johnson in her peripheral vision

"What's your name?" Johnson barked.

Olivia stared at him tight-lipped.

"Where's your ID? Maybe I need to see your name

and address. Maybe you need to be kept in line." Johnson's body leaned forward to menace Olivia.

When the huge man made a move to grab Olivia's arm, she side-stepped to keep him from reaching into her pocket to get her ID, afraid that if he found out her address, he might come after her.

"Who are you?" Olivia asked. "Why are you bothering us?"

"I own this gym." Johnson glowered.

Olivia knew he was lying, but didn't want to call him on it so she pretended she believed him. "My friend is sick. She had too much to drink. Her boyfriend just broke up with her," Olivia lied. Her body trembled under Johnson's dark gaze. "We've been driving around. We want to join a gym. We came by to see if anyone was here to give us information."

"It's eleven at night," Johnson growled.

"We heard the gym was open twenty-four, seven," Olivia said.

"Where'd you hear that?"

Olivia's eyes flashed. "What's your name? Is this really your gym? We aren't doing anything wrong." She took a small step towards the hulking man trying hard to project confidence and authority to prove she wasn't intimidated.

"If you want to join the gym, then why are you at the back of the building?" Johnson demanded.

"I told you," Olivia said. "My friend had too much to drink. I brought her back here to throw up."

"Maybe I'll call the cops," Johnson said. "You're trespassing."

Olivia took another step forward. "Go ahead. Call them. I'll tell them you hit me and broke my phone. That will be good advertising for your lousy gym."

Olivia thought Johnson was about to strike her, so she bent down to speak to Ynes before he could decide to act on his impulse.

"Are you feeling okay?" Olivia asked Ynes. "Come on, let's get out of here." Slipping her hand under Ynes' arm, she tugged to help her stand. "Let's go home." Olivia bent to pick up her phone and then led Ynes away from Johnson hoping like heck that he wouldn't try to stop them.

Ynes said, "I think I'm going to be sick." She coughed, and staggered, keeping up her drunken act.

"The car's just around the corner," Olivia said. They kept walking.

"Don't let me catch you back here again," Johnson's voice boomed.

"Don't worry," Olivia called back to him. "We won't be joining your awful gym."

The girls rounded the corner of the building. There was a shiny black Mercedes G-class SUV parked right next to Ynes' car. When they reached their vehicle, Olivia opened the passenger side door and helped

Ynes to sit. Hurrying to the driver's side, she flung open the door and hopped into the driver's seat, immediately hitting the button to lock the doors.

Ynes handed her companion the car key. "Let's get out of here before I really do get sick," she said.

Olivia turned the key in the ignition, put the car in reverse, and backed out of the spot. She shifted into drive and stomped the gas pedal. "Keep your eye on the mirrors, make sure Johnson isn't following us. I almost had a stroke back there."

Ynes said, "No one would ever know it. You ever think of going into acting? My hands will never stop shaking."

"My whole body is shaking," Olivia said. "We're idiots. This was a stupid idea. Let's leave investigating crimes to the police."

"Wait until I tell Eva that Adam Johnson showed up...and what he was doing in there," Ynes said. "She'll die."

Olivia said, "Text Melissa. Tell her we're okay. Have her meet us back at the apartment." She made a right turn out of the industrial area. "That Johnson guy is trouble. Drug dealing. Pushing us around. Threatening Gary. Possibly a murderer. What a piece of work." Beads of sweat rolled down the side of her face.

"We can't tell the police we saw the drug deal," Ynes said. "Johnson will know we saw the whole thing. He'll know it was us who told."

"I don't want to tell the police either. I'm such a wimp. I wish I was brave." Olivia sighed and shook her head. "Johnson is a monster. I almost passed out dealing with that horrible excuse for a human being. We're lucky he didn't hurt us. We should get pepper spray."

"Yeah," Ynes said. "Or, a gun."

Olivia said, "And anyway, if we did talk to the police, we'd have to explain how we happened to be in the gym when it was closed." She wished there was a way to alert the police that Johnson was selling drugs without calling attention to Ynes and herself. It didn't sit well with her that people had to fear others or that some could get away with illegal activities. "Tell your friend Eva what we heard him doing. She should know he's selling drugs out of the gym. She needs to avoid Johnson and keep herself safe."

After a drive that seemed to take hours, Olivia turned the car onto her street and slowed to find a parking space.

"Don't bother parking my car," Ynes said. "I'm just going to drive home."

"Why don't you come up?" Olivia asked. "We can tell Melissa what happened. Have some tea or a glass of wine."

Ynes shook her head. "Thanks, but I'm exhausted. I'm just going to drive home and get into bed."

Olivia stopped Ynes' car next to the sidewalk in

front of her building. "Is there anything we can do to get the police after Johnson?"

Ynes let out a sigh. "No, and I don't want to get killed." She gave Olivia a look. "Not now, anyway. Not over this."

Olivia nodded. "I'll talk to you later." She got out and stood on the sidewalk while Ynes came around from the passenger side. They hugged.

Ynes got into her car, put the window down, and leaned out. "By the way, you're wrong," Ynes told Olivia. "You're one of the bravest people I know." She started the engine, pulled away from the curb, and drove down the street.

Olivia watched her go, feeling worried and unsettled, and not one tiny bit brave. Anxiety pulsed through her body. Not only did she feel badly that they'd failed at the mission, but she berated herself for being so foolish to have put themselves at risk. They very well might have ended up getting hurt tonight, or worse. If only they'd been able to get some information on Johnson that might have tied him to the murders.

With shoulders slumped, Olivia turned and slowly climbed the stairs to the front door of her apartment building.

The bad guy wins.

16

Olivia pushed the library door open and exited into the brisk October night, her high brown ponytail swinging as she walked. She'd spent four hours researching and writing and her eyes felt like dry orbs aching in their sockets. All she wanted was a nice hot shower and something to eat.

A familiar figured lurked in her peripheral vision, and when she turned to look, her heart sank. Kayla was sitting on the stone wall that lined the edge of the walkway. A heavy wool jacket hid her slender build and a knit hat covered her short blonde hair.

Olivia realized she didn't have the strength to put up with any nonsense and hoped for a second that it was someone else sitting on the wall, someone who just looked like Kayla.

Kayla jumped down from her perch and approached Olivia.

Olivia stood there, her expression blank, wishing she was home in her pajamas. *No such luck.*

"Do you have some time?" Kayla asked.

"I was heading home. What's up?" Olivia tried not to sound like she was dreading the encounter.

"Can we go someplace? To talk?"

"Now?" Olivia asked.

"Yes, now."

Olivia wanted to say no, but instead she said, "There's a coffee place on Main Street. It's open late." *Why can't I ever just say no?* Her heart sinking, she wondered how long she would have to be out with Kayla.

Kayla nodded and they turned to head to Main Street. Neither one said a word for two blocks.

"How'd you know I was in the library?" Olivia asked.

"You're always in there."

"Not always."

"I watched your building for a while. I didn't see you, so I figured you must be in the second most likely place," Kayla said.

Olivia sighed. "Were you going to sit there all night?"

"No. Only until, you came out. I didn't think you'd sleep in there."

Olivia suppressed a grin. "Why the impromptu visit?"

"I'll tell you when we get there."

They walked a few more blocks, and then entered the coffee shop. The lighting was soft, the wood floors gleamed. A glass case held desserts, cookies, pies, cakes, scones. The scents of hazelnut coffee, melted chocolate, and cinnamon floated on the air. Olivia's stomach growled.

"I'm starving. I have to get something to eat before we talk," Olivia told Kayla.

Kayla moved to a side corner table and sat while Olivia ordered a tea and a giant slice of chocolate mousse cake.

Olivia joined Kayla at the table and placed her dessert in the center.

"Have some."

"I'm not hungry." Kayla pulled the knit cap off her head and put it in her lap.

Olivia removed her jacket, hung it on the back of her seat, and sat down. She placed a forkful of the mousse cake into her mouth and nearly swooned. "Okay. I can talk now." She took another bite of the cake and mumbled, "What's up?"

"The police came to talk to me."

Olivia's eyes went wide. She held the fork in the air. "Why?"

"They got an anonymous tip that I was in the apartment the night of the murders."

Olivia's brow furrowed. "You think I told the police? You think I called them?"

Kayla sat stone-faced.

"I didn't," Olivia said. "It wasn't me."

"Melissa then," Kayla said.

Olivia shook her head. "No, she didn't. Why would we do that?"

"Because maybe you think I'm the killer."

Olivia placed her fork on the plate. She didn't know what to believe so she didn't say anything.

"So you *do* think I did it."

Olivia stared at Kayla for a few beats. "Where do you live in Cambridge?" she asked.

"In Central Square," Kayla said.

"How were you outside Jack Wilson's building the night he was murdered?"

Kayla bit her lip. Her eyes blinked fast a few times. "I went to Somerville that night to walk by Christian's apartment. I stood across the street from his building and stared up at his windows. I missed him. I just can't believe he's gone." She picked up Olivia's mug of tea and took a long drink from it. She swallowed hard. "Some people walked by while I was standing there. I heard them say someone else had been killed. I followed them to hear more. They ended up outside Jack's place."

"What did the cops ask you when they brought you in for questioning?" Olivia asked.

"They asked if I was in the apartment the night of the murders. What did I see? Why didn't I come forward? Did I go to school? Where did I work? Stuff like that." Her expression clouded over. "I didn't like it. They made me feel like I was guilty."

"Did you tell them the truth?"

"Yes, but I should've lied about some things."

"Like what?" Olivia asked her.

"I told them where I went to school. What I study," Kayla said.

Olivia's face was puzzled.

"I go to the North Street School."

"That's a wonderful school," Olivia said. "Why should you lie about that?"

"I'm studying to be a locksmith."

"That'll be a great career." As soon as she made the comment, Olivia realized why Kayla thought she should have lied about her schooling. "Oh. The cops think you used your skills to break into Jack's building?"

"They didn't come right out and say that, but I know what they were implying."

"How did the interview end? Did they accuse you?"

"No. They told me they might want to speak with me again though. They suggested I stick around the area." Kayla lifted a forkful of Olivia's cake to her mouth.

"Do you want your own fork?" Olivia asked.

Kayla shrugged.

"Do you think you should get a lawyer?"

"Do you know one?" Kayla asked.

"My aunt's a lawyer, but she doesn't handle cases like this. She could refer you to someone."

"I don't think I need one. Not yet, anyway," Kayla said. She finished Olivia's tea. "So if you and your sidekick didn't tell the police that I was in Christian's apartment, who did? Luke?"

"I don't think he would, but I can't say for certain," Olivia said.

Kayla said, "Eric got Luke angry the other night. Would that make Luke call the police? To get back at me? To get back at Eric? Does Luke think I did it?"

"I don't know. Maybe you should talk to Luke. I don't know him well enough to be able to say if he would call the police or not. Who else knows you were there that night?"

"I thought just you three did," Kayla said. "And, Eric."

"Somebody else must have seen you there."

"Well, who the heck could it be?" Kayla mumbled, trying to think of who might have seen her at Christian's that night.

Olivia considered something, not sure if she should

ask, but went ahead with it. "You were arrested for assault?"

Kayla's eyes widened. "How do you know that?"

"Eric told us."

Kayla's lips pressed together. "Why the heck did he tell you that?"

"He wants us to stay away from you. He doesn't want us dragging you into it. He explained that you didn't want to go to the police because you had a record." Olivia paused for a few seconds. "Why were you arrested?"

"I'm not telling you that." Kayla looked like she wanted to run away.

"Eric said you had an abusive boyfriend."

"Jeez." Kayla was fuming. "Has he ever heard of privacy?"

"Was your boyfriend abusive to you?"

Kayla's eyes flashed around the room. "That hasn't got anything to do with my life today."

Olivia was quiet.

"I'm not talking about the past," Kayla said.

"Okay," Olivia said. She kept her face neutral.

"I don't have a record. The charges were dropped," Kayla said.

"Okay."

Kayla cocked her head, hesitated for a moment, and then asked, "You think I killed them, don't you?"

"It's a weird coincidence isn't it?" Olivia's tone was thoughtful.

"What is?" Kayla's lips were tight. A muscle in her cheek twitched.

"That you and the killer had ski masks on that night."

Kayla stiffened. "What are you implying? That there were two killers? That I'm one of them?" Her voice shook.

Olivia shrugged, and then she shook her head. "I'm not implying anything. Really. I'm just thinking out loud." Olivia just couldn't picture Kayla as a killer. There was something about her. She couldn't quite put her finger on it. Something, under the spiked hair and tough exterior ... there was something vulnerable, and almost sweet. Olivia also knew that she could be misperceiving everything about Kayla and could be very wrong about what she might be capable of. Olivia gave herself a mental shake. "It's just a very odd coincidence, isn't it?"

Kayla said nothing. Her woolen cap had flattened her usual spikey hair. It hung in soft wisps over her forehead. A pink flush colored her porcelain skin.

Something had been picking at the back of Olivia's mind, but try as she
might, she just couldn't bring it to the forefront. She exhaled a long breath and studied Kayla's face. Olivia held her hand out for the fork, Kayla passed it to

her, and she speared a chunk of cake and placed it in her mouth. She chewed, swallowed, and said, "Did you want Christian dead? For breaking up with you?"

Kayla blinked. "Well, yeah. Sometimes. He hurt me."

Olivia raised her eyes to Kayla. It was an honest answer. Wouldn't lots of people say they wished ill to the person who hurt them? But, not really mean it.

"*That* probably isn't something you should reveal to the police if they interview you again."

Kayla said, "Oh, I never would have hurt him. You know how it is. One day you wish he would get run over by a bus and the next day you imagine how you'd forgive him with open arms when he comes running back to you saying what a terrible mistake he made."

Olivia knew exactly what Kayla meant.

Ever since she was a toddler, Olivia and her aunt spent every summer in Ogunquit, Maine. From the time she was a little kid until she was fourteen, she whiled away every summer day hanging out with her best friend, Brad. They would bike and swim and kayak and lay in the grass reading under the apple tree. When they were fourteen, Brad developed a crush on a new girl and abandoned Olivia for the last two weeks of summer in order to moon over the newcomer.

Olivia would sit in the rocking chair on the small porch of the house, imagining terrible things happening to Brad and his "mistake" like capsizing in their kayaks and drowning in the ocean. She pictured Brad as he took his last breath, realizing the error of his ways and wishing he could see Olivia one last time.

After that year, Brad's family decided not to summer in Maine anymore and that was last she ever saw of Brad. Thinking of him, a little twinge squeezed Olivia's heart.

Funny. To still miss someone after all these years.

Kayla turned to the window and looked out at the lights of the city twinkling in the darkness. A wistful smile played at the corner of her mouth. "Christian was just so great." Her face took on a look of immense sadness. "He's gone. It's time for me to stop pretending that I'll wake up from all this and he'll come back to me."

17

Olivia came out of the bedroom dressed in a black cocktail dress and black heels. The sleeveless dress had a high neck and the fabric followed the trim lines of her body ending several inches above the knee. She had her hair styled the way she usually did for a more formal party, with it half up and half down, gentle waves falling just past her shoulders. Olivia didn't usually wear much makeup, just some mascara and lip gloss, but tonight she had applied a smudge of eyeliner and a bit of blush.

Melissa sat in the easy chair in the living room fiddling with the small buckle on the strap of her heels. "I can't get this thing tight enough. There, I pushed it through." She looked up at Olivia. "Wow. You look great. That dress fits perfectly." Melissa stood. She had on an emerald green cocktail dress with spaghetti straps over the shoulders. A necklace of blue and green stones encircled her neck and she wore dark green heels. She'd curled her long, nearly black hair and the waves settled around her shoulders and cascaded down her back.

"Damn. You look like a movie star." Olivia smiled. "You're like four inches taller than usual. Now you're my height," she kidded her petite friend.

Melissa ignored Olivia's teasing and grabbed her clutch and a sweater. "Come on, let's go dazzle some guys."

Olivia put on a short, black jacket and the two went down to the street to the waiting cab. They rode across Cambridge, over the bridge that crossed the Charles River, and into the center of Boston, where the cab stopped in front of a swanky hotel. The college and university formal event was held in a different hotel ballroom each year and drawing both undergraduate and graduate students from many area schools, it sold out annually. The young women joined couples and groups of friends as they entered the lobby and made their way to the ballroom.

Cut-glass chandeliers cast a warm glow over the crowd. The room was decorated with flowers, pumpkins, and tiny white lights and tables were laden with appetizers and desserts. Waiters carrying trays of hors d'oeuvres wove around the groups of people who stood together chatting and laughing. A bar was set up on one side of the room and a DJ played on a stage at the rear. Music pulsed in the air and a large number of people danced on the wood floor in front of the stage.

"What a crowd," Melissa smiled. "This is going to be fun."

The young women milled about until they found some friends standing on the other side of the room. Olivia thought how great it was that people were out having a good time together knowing that many of them needed a break from the sorrow and horror of recent events. It would be helpful to have a reprieve from things for a short while. Olivia and Melissa joined their friends on the dance floor and stayed there for almost an hour.

Olivia grabbed Melissa's arm and said, "I'm going to get a cold drink."

Melissa decided to get something, too, so they approached the line in front of the bar. Four guys stood to the side talking and two of them joined the young women at the back of the line to strike up a conversation.

Olivia could feel her heart start to beat a little faster when the tall, athletically-built blonde man with blue eyes stood next to her. The other guy was fit, but a bit huskier with longer dark hair and hazel green eyes. They introduced themselves and shared where and what they were studying.

"I'm doing my doctorate in chemical engineering at Boston University," the blond guy named Jason told them.

"Where did you do your undergraduate work?" Melissa asked.

"MIT."

"We have some friends studying at MIT," Olivia said. "Do you know Luke Smithson?"

"No, I don't. Different department no doubt," Jason said. "Although even in the same department we all don't know each other. What are you studying, Olivia?" He smiled at her and held her eyes.

"I'm finishing my degree in international relations and I'll be applying to law school soon."

"Do you have a first choice of law school?"

"Not really. It would be nice to be admitted to one of the schools in the Boston area though. I'd like to stay in Massachusetts."

After finishing drinks, Jason and Olivia, and Melissa and John, took to the floor in front of the DJ and mixed in with the throng of dancers enjoying the latest hits.

Olivia and Jason danced to a number of songs before deciding to take a break and find a table to sit at and talk, so they moved away from the crowded dance floor and saw some people that Olivia knew. The group called them over and Olivia and Jason sat with them and chatted. A guy that Olivia didn't know introduced himself to her.

"Nick," he said shaking her hand. "I graduated last year. Now I'm working for a start up in Kendall Square."

"Which one?" Olivia asked. "We have friends working in Kendall."

"LearnApp. We do educational products for middle school kids."

The company name sounded familiar to Olivia and then she placed it. "I met someone recently who had worked there. He got laid off."

"Really? Who?"

"His name is Eric. I don't know his last name."

Nick's face went serious. "Eric Daniels?"

"Maybe."

"How do you know him?" Nick asked.

"I met him through a friend. I don't know him well at all," Olivia said.

"Then you're lucky." Nick scowled.

"Why?"

"He was a problem. Things would set him off. Sometimes he was friendly, a nice guy, then he would turn nasty. He'd say mean things to people. He didn't work well with the rest of the people at the company."

"So they laid him off?"

"Well...." the guy shrugged.

"He got fired?" Olivia asked.

"One day, out of the blue, he stormed into the CEO's office, ranting about a co-worker. The CEO had to call the building security. It was all about nothing. Eric had a fit over some difference of opinion with someone. Nobody wanted to work with him because of his moods. He was volatile."

"Wow," Olivia said. "I wonder if this is the same Eric."

"I think it must be. Nobody's been laid off at our company."

Olivia thought over what she had just heard.

Nick said, "Eric's like some technical genius. I always thought he should be working for the government, CIA or something. But with his temper and personality, that'd be out of the question. Eric wants to do everything his own way. He's not a team player. I don't think he'll be working at any startups anytime soon. People know each other around here. Word gets out."

Olivia nodded. "I only met him in passing." She craned her neck to see if she could find Melissa. She wanted to tell her what this guy had just shared. "I'm going to go look for my friend. Nice talking with you." She stood and headed off to find Melissa.

"Olivia." Good looking Jason called to her. "You're not leaving are you?"

"I'm going to find Melissa."

"Can I come with you?"

"I'll be back," she told him. She didn't know if she would be back. Jason made her slightly uncomfortable. Somehow she got the feeling that he might be possessive. Olivia had so much to do with schoolwork and law school applications that she wasn't sure she wanted to get involved with anyone. She spotted Melissa coming out of the bathroom.

"Mel," Olivia called to her.

Melissa smiled and walked over to meet her friend. "How's it going with Blondie?"

"He's okay. He might be a pain. I haven't decided yet."

Melissa laughed.

"What about the guy you were dancing with?" Olivia asked.

"I get the feeling he has a girlfriend."

Olivia rolled her eyes. "Listen to what a guy I just met said about Eric."

"Kayla's Eric?"

"Yes." Olivia proceeded to tell Melissa all of the details. "The guy should never have spilled so much about Eric, but I think he's had a few too many drinks so he told me all of that stuff."

"That's wild. But actually, I believe it. Didn't you get the feeling something was weird with Eric? He's so...I don't know ... angry? Controlling?"

"Yeah. The way he was so critical of Christian even though he had only met him once," Olivia said.

"But I suppose he was just looking out for his friend."

"He's still odd," Melissa said. "Speaking of one too many drinks, I think I've had enough for the night."

"You want to go home?"

"I'm starting to feel sick," Melissa said.

"Let's get out of here, then." Olivia took Melissa's arm, went to pick up their things, and then headed for the exit. "Just don't throw up in the cab."

OLIVIA PAID the cab driver and the girls stepped out onto the dark sidewalk in front of their building. When they reached the front stairs, someone called out to Olivia, and they turned towards the voice, startled.

Jason from the formal dance was sitting on the hood of his parked car, a bright red Porsche 911 convertible. He hopped off the hood and leaned back against the front of the automobile, smiling. "You didn't say goodbye," he said to Olivia.

Olivia bristled at how forward Jason was. "Good-bye," she said.

Jason laughed. "I could have given you a ride home, you know."

"Three of us in that thing?" Olivia asked, and then her face hardened. "How did you know where we live? Did you go through my purse?"

Jason chuckled and shook his head. "Of course, not. I just asked around."

Olivia didn't like that Jason had shown up at her apartment uninvited.

"I wanted to be sure you made it home safe," he said. "There's been trouble around here recently."

"Well, thanks. We made it home." Olivia couldn't help the scowl on her face.

Melissa stood silently listening to the back and forth banter.

"Can I come up?" Jason asked. He took a step away from his car.

"No," Olivia said, exasperated.

"Another time?"

"Jason, we're tired. It feels weird that you're sitting outside my building. It's creepy almost."

"I think it's kind of nice that he found you," Melissa said.

Olivia glared at her.

"I think you should listen to your friend." Jason grinned at Olivia.

"I'm going in and going to bed." Olivia tried to banish the annoyance from her tone. "It was considerate of you to make sure we got home." She took Melissa's elbow and turned her to the stairs.

"Can I have your number?" Jason asked.

"I'm sure you'll be able to find it on your own," Olivia told him without looking back. "Goodnight."

Olivia unlocked the front door. Melissa pulled off her heels and the two of them trudged up the stairs to their apartment.

"He seems sweet," Melissa said.

"He just wanted to be sure I saw that car of his. He's showing off. He seems like a stalker," Olivia said. "The word 'pushy' also comes to mind."

"Along with the words cute and fit and wealthy," Melissa chuckled.

"I'm just not in the mood for his antics," Olivia said. "I'm exhausted and unsettled and I feel like I can't think straight these days. I don't have the energy to deal with him or to start something new."

They reached the landing in front of their door.

"Are those stairs getting steeper?" Melissa asked as she leaned against the wall puffing while Olivia fumbled for her key. "I think you should go out with him if he calls."

Olivia made a face as she stuck the key in the lock and turned it.

"He might be a nice distraction from all this mess that's been happening," Melissa said.

Olivia pushed the door open. "A nice distraction or a pain in my butt?"

18

Olivia, Melissa, Ynes, and several others of Melissa's friends left the "T" station and walked to the South End club. It was Melissa's birthday and the group had just left a restaurant on Boston's Boylston Street where they had gathered for the birthday dinner. The group of friends wanted to extend the celebration and decided to head to some clubs for dancing. Melissa had been slightly subdued during dinner.

Olivia walked beside her friend. "You okay? You seem sort of quiet tonight."

"I'm okay. I feel like I might be coming down with a cold or something, but I'm having fun." Melissa put her arm through Olivia's as they strolled along. "It's nice to be all together just hanging out for the night."

Olivia said, "Did you text Luke to tell him where we're headed?"

"Yeah, he said he was done in the lab and would head out in a few minutes to go home to change and then he'd meet us."

The group entered the club and found a table, then pulled extra chairs up to it and squished around. A waitress came by and took drink orders. A few of the friends sat and chatted while the rest got up to dance.

Sitting at the table, Melissa said to Olivia, "I'm feeling warm."

Olivia touched her friend's forehead. "I don't think you have a fever."

"Do you have some aspirin?"

"I changed to a smaller purse and left the aspirin at home," Olivia told her. "You want me to go get you some? We passed a convenience store a block from here."

"Maybe. You wouldn't mind?" Melissa asked. "I don't want to go home. I want to stay out with every-one. A couple of aspirins might make me feel better."

"No worries. Sit tight. I'll be right back." Olivia smiled.

"I'll go with you," Ynes told her. "It's getting late. I don't want you walking around alone."

The two women left Melissa talking with another friend and they exited the club to run the brief errand. It only took ten minutes to get to the store and purchase the aspirin. As they headed back and approached the club, they heard a female voice cry out from the parking area at the rear of the building.

"What was that?" Ynes stopped and looked around for the source of the shout.

"Is someone in trouble or are they joking around?" Olivia asked, peering down the side street that led to the club's parking lot.

A scream pierced the air. Ynes and Olivia exchanged a quick glance and took off running towards the parking lot.

"There!" Ynes pointed at a guy looming over a young woman in between two parked vehicles. The guy had one hand on her chest. His other hand held tight to the girl's long hair yanking her head back. The man's mouth was clamped over her lips. The woman squirmed and pushed at the tall, husky guy.

Ynes yelled at the man. "Let her go!"

Olivia shouted that she was calling the cops. She punched "911" into her phone and reported the incident as she and Ynes got closer.

The guy looked up and when he saw Ynes and Olivia, he whirled, recognition flashing over his face. "You two!"

Olivia and Ynes were face to face with Adam Johnson. The woman he had been harassing clutched at her ripped blouse and took off, crying.

"You two interfering cows," Johnson growled, his face contorted in anger. He lunged at them.

Olivia side-stepped away from the man, but her ankle twisted and she went down hard on her butt. Johnson grabbed Olivia's hair with one hand and tried to yank her to her feet. His other meaty paw clamped around her neck.

Gasping for breath, Olivia clawed at Johnson's hand.

A second later, Johnson suddenly released his grip. By the time Olivia's mind processed what had happened, it was done and Johnson was doubled over clutching his gut. The man dropped to his knees, sucking air into his lungs in rasping gulps.

Ynes had struck Johnson so swiftly with her hands and feet that Olivia only registered the attack on the hulking athlete as a complete blur. Sitting on the concrete, her eyes were wide and her mouth hung open as she rubbed her neck where Johnson had gripped and choked her. Ynes reached down to take Olivia's hand to help her up.

"Don't ask," Ynes said.

"Really? How can I not ask? What the heck was that? How did you do that?" Olivia questioned her.

A police car flew down the street and pulled to an abrupt halt several yards away from the two young women and the still gasping Johnson. One officer approached Johnson and another came up to the two friends.

Olivia and Ynes explained how they heard screams and found Johnson attacking a young woman who fled when they approached. They reported that Johnson wheeled on them and that he knocked Olivia to the ground and tried to choke her.

"She attacked me," Johnson yelped, rising to his feet, pointing at Ynes, but still gripping his stomach.

The officers gave him a look of disgust. One of the officers asked for Ynes,' Olivia's, and Johnson's identification and the other officer took the young women off to the side and told them to wait for a few minutes. He went to the squad car and sat in the driver's seat.

"He must be calling in our ID info," Ynes said.

Olivia was still rubbing at her neck.

After a few minutes, the officer returned and put cuffs on Johnson who began to rant and swear. The police told Olivia and Ynes that they could go, but that an officer would contact them again at a later time. A second squad car rocketed into the parking lot as Olivia and Ynes were heading for the sidewalk. A crowd of people had gathered to watch.

"Are you okay?" Ynes asked Olivia as they headed to the entrance to the club.

"Yeah. I'll probably be sore tomorrow though. Especially, my butt." She rubbed her tailbone.

"I can't believe it was Adam Johnson," Ynes said. "That monster."

"Where did you learn to do whatever it was you did to Johnson?"

"I took martial arts classes in high school."

Olivia's eyebrows went up. "You learned to do that in high school? What kind of high school was it? A military academy?"

Ynes opened the door to the club and paused for Olivia to enter first. Pulsing music blared inside.

"Why didn't you tell me about your skill when we were at the gym the other night?" Olivia asked. "I wouldn't have been so nervous if I knew I had the Karate Kid with me."

Ynes rolled her eyes. "It's not that helpful against someone with a gun." She placed her hand on the small of Olivia's back and gave her a playful nudge. "Go tell Melissa who we ran into in the parking lot. I'm going to the bathroom." Before they parted ways, Ynes locked eyes with Olivia and said, "And I wouldn't mind if you didn't tell anyone about what I did to Johnson."

"I don't keep secrets from Melissa, but, I won't tell anyone else."

Olivia delivered the aspirin to Melissa and told the group of friends about what transpired in the parking lot and who was involved, but she left out Ynes' heroics. Olivia practically had to shout over the music. Two guys in their group of friends hurried outside to see what was going on with Johnson and the police.

Something in Olivia's subconscious picked at her causing some unexplained anxiety to flow through her body while she was sitting with her friends around the table.

"I can't believe you ran into Johnson," Melissa said. "What are the odds of that?" She swallowed two of the aspirins that Olivia had bought for her.

"How are you feeling?" Olivia asked. "Are you worse?"

"I'm achy and my throat's sore. I hope I'm not getting the flu. I have too much work to do."

Ynes returned to the table as Olivia placed her hand against Melissa's forehead and then touched her cheek. "You feel warm now. You must be coming down with a fever. Maybe you should call it a night?"

Melissa groaned. The friends who had stepped out to see what was happening with Johnson rushed back to the table.

"The cops arrested Adam Johnson," one friend blurted.

"People in the crowd said the cops searched the trunk of Johnson's car and found a bunch of guns and a knife with traces of blood inside a backpack," the second friend said.

Other friends piped up with tidbits of information.

"I read in the news that Johnson's girlfriend has a restraining order on him."

"Yeah. I heard he's a suspect in a murder case in Florida."

Melissa, Olivia, and Ynes exchanged glances. Ynes leaned towards them. "Maybe the knife the cops found will tie Johnson to Christian and Gary?"

"Maybe the case is about to be solved," Olivia said. She felt hopeful for the first time in days. Turning to Melissa, she saw beads of sweat on her friend's pale face. "You don't look so good. We need to go home."

"I don't feel so good. I guess you're right." Melissa's eyelids were half-closed.

"I'll call a cab," Ynes said. "You don't want to take public transport home when

you're feeling sick."

The three said goodnight to the other friends and Olivia took Melissa's arm and helped her to the door.

"Everybody must think I'm drunk," Melissa moaned.

Melissa started to shiver when they stood outside in the chilly night air waiting for the cab. Olivia offered Melissa her coat, but she declined. Olivia rubbed her friend's shoulders and Melissa leaned heavily against her.

Shuffling her feet to keep warm, Ynes said, "Where's that damn cab?"

Suddenly, what had been pricking at Olivia came

into her mind. "Melissa, Luke never showed up. Did he text you?" she asked.

Melissa shook her head. "I texted him again when you went to get the aspirin. He never answered."

Olivia shot a concerned look at Ynes. "He said he was meeting us at the club. I'm calling him. Hold on to Melissa." She punched at her phone's screen, lifted it to her ear, and waited. She shook her head. "He doesn't answer."

"Maybe he's on his way." Melissa's voice was just above a whisper. She could barely keep her eyes open. "Maybe he's on the "T" and doesn't have cell phone reception."

"Maybe." Olivia looked at Ynes, worry etched over her face. "Maybe, not?"

"I know what you're thinking," Ynes said. There was a tinge of urgency to her voice.

Olivia said to Ynes, "Will you go inside and get Amy? She can take Melissa home. You and I can take a cab to Luke's."

Ynes ran into the club and returned several minutes later with Amy. A cab pulled up to the curb. "I know you're sick," Ynes said to Melissa, "but Olivia and I need to take this one. Amy will call for another a cab to take you home."

Olivia hugged Melissa and followed Ynes into the cab. They gave the driver Luke's address and the taxi pulled into the traffic.

"We're probably wrong," Olivia said, trying to convince herself. "Luke's fine."

"Better safe than sorry," Ynes told her.

Olivia's heart had dropped into her stomach. She pulled out her phone and called Luke again. "Ugh. Still no answer." Her hand shook as she slipped the phone back into her pocket. Olivia tried to reduce the tension she was feeling by taking slow breaths. "He's probably at home with some girl and we'll come banging on his door." She forced a smile.

Ynes flicked her eyes to Olivia. "Let's hope so."

The cab stopped at the curb, the girls paid, and leaped out. They rushed to Luke's building, ran up the steps, and pressed on the button to ring Luke's apartment. Olivia jammed her finger against the button over and over. Tears gathered in her eyes. "He's not answering."

"Try another apartment," Ynes said. "Push any button."

Olivia pushed a different one. A voice came over the intercom. "Who is it?"

Ynes said, "We're trying to reach our friend. Luke Smithson. He's in '212.' He isn't answering. We're worried about him..." She was about to go on with her explanation when the door buzzed and Olivia grabbed the handle and flung it open. They tore up the stairs and when they reached the landing, they halted.

Ynes gasped.

Luke lay crumpled on his side on the floor in front of his open apartment door. Blood flowed from a red gash in his throat. The front of his jacket was cut. Blood stained the leather and dripped onto the floor. The skin of his hands was red with blood.

Kneeling next to him, holding a knife, was Kayla.

19

"Olivia," Kayla whispered.

"Kayla, drop the knife," Olivia said gently, unsure of what Kayla might do. She took a step forward.

Kayla blinked and looked down at the knife in her hand. She shook her head and raised her eyes to Olivia. She let the knife slip from her grasp. "I didn't do this."

Olivia knelt beside Luke and touched his neck to locate a pulse. She kept Kayla in her peripheral vision. "He's alive." Her voice quavered as she turned to Ynes. "Call 911." Shrugging out of her jacket, she pulled her sweater over her head, balled it up, and pressed it against Luke's abdomen.

"Luke, can you hear me?" Olivia asked. Luke lay motionless and did not respond. She could see defensive wounds on his hands. "We're here, Luke," she spoke to him soothingly. "You'll be okay. Help's on the way. We're with you." The words hitched in her throat and tears dropped from her eyes.

Kayla knelt behind Luke. Tears spilled down her cheeks while she leaned to check his neck wound. She lifted her scarf from around her shoulders and used it to apply pressure to the gash in Luke's neck.

Keeping her hands firmly pressing the sweater against Luke's stomach wounds, Olivia shifted to look at Kayla.

Kayla's breath was coming in shallow gasps like she was close to hyperventilating. "I just got here. He was on the floor. I heard you coming up the steps. I grabbed the knife. I was afraid the attacker was coming back."

Olivia didn't know whether to believe Kayla or not. "Why did you come to his apartment?"

"Luke and I have met up a few times. For coffee, a drink, to talk about Christian and Gary and everything that's been going on. He said he was going to meet a bunch of you at a club tonight. He asked me to go." Kayla's eyes bored into Olivia's. "I didn't do this. He was like this when I got here. Olivia, I swear it's true."

"How did you get into the building?" Olivia asked, adjusting her hands on Luke's abdomen for maximum pressure.

Anxiety washed over Kayla's face. "Probably the

same way you did. I pushed someone else's door buzzer and asked to be let in." She leaned back from Luke's prone form. "God, I know how this looks. You think I stabbed him. The police will think so, too."

She scooted a few inches away on her butt and stood.

"Don't leave, Kayla," Olivia warned.

Ynes knelt and took over for Kayla, pressing on the scarf to stay the flow of blood from Luke's neck. "If you take off, it will look bad. Stay here. Just tell the police what happened."

Kayla's eyes darted around the hallway as she tried to make a decision. A siren could be heard close by.

"Don't run," Olivia said. "If you're innocent, you need to stay and tell what happened. If you take off, it will make you look guilty."

"Don't tell the police I was here," Kayla said, stepping back. "Please." Her voice shook.

"Your fingerprints are on the knife," Olivia said.

Kayla froze. Her hands clutched the sides of her head. Her muscles seemed to give out and she slipped down hard on the floor.

The front door of the building opened. Heavy feet could be heard on the steps.

"We're up here," Ynes called out.

A police officer and two emergency medical workers appeared on the landing. The EMTs raced to Luke's side and Ynes and Olivia backed away. Kayla was still sitting on the floor with her head pressed against her knees.

"There's a knife on the floor," Olivia told the cop.

Another officer climbed the stairs. "Move back down the hall," he ordered the women.

"Kayla," Olivia said, placing her hand on the young woman's shoulder. "Come on. Stand up. We need to move down the hallway." She placed her hand under Kayla's arm and tugged. Dazed, Kayla stood and moved with Ynes and Olivia.

Luke was placed on a stretcher and carried down the stairs and into the waiting ambulance.

Each woman talked individually with a detective who appeared shortly after the initial arrival of the two officers and the EMTs. Their names and addresses were collected along with their accounts of why they were there and what they saw when they came on the scene.

Olivia was the last to speak with the detective and by the time she was finished and allowed to leave, she dragged herself down the stairs to the first floor and stepped out the door. Ynes was sitting on the front steps waiting. She looked up when the door opened.

"Where's Kayla?" Olivia asked. She sat down on the concrete step next to Ynes, the spot illuminated by a streetlight. The night air was cold and Olivia pulled her coat closer around herself.

Ynes said, "She was gone when I came out."

Olivia looked at the blood on her hands. Ynes took hand sanitizer and some tissues out of her purse and handed them to Olivia, who took them and cleaned her skin.

Olivia felt like all her energy had drained out of her body, so she put her arms around her legs and rested her head on her knees. "At least Luke is alive." Tears welled in her eyes. "I thought all this was over. The cops arrested Adam Johnson tonight. They found a knife in his trunk. I thought these killings were over and done. Now, Luke is attacked. It can't have been Johnson. He can't be responsible for killing the guys." She sounded so weary. "Poor Luke. I can't believe this happened. Who's doing this? Why?"

"What do you think?" Ynes asked. "You believe Kayla's story? She had nothing to do with this?"

Olivia lifted her head. "I don't know. Why would she try to kill Luke?"

"She might think he could identify her because he saw her in Christian's apartment that night."

"But, Luke didn't see the killer's face and Kayla claims she didn't see much at all. Just someone's feet."

"So she claims," Ynes said, skeptically. "She could be lying about hiding in that bedroom. She might be the one who killed them."

"I don't know. I don't think she's lying. I don't think she did it."

"Reasons?" Ynes asked.

Olivia lifted her palms up and shrugged. "Intuition, feelings?" She blinked at Ynes. "Am I wrong about her?"

Ynes scowled. "I think she did it."

Olivia sighed. "We should go to the hospital. See about Luke."

"I'll call a cab. Again," Ynes said. She reached into her pocket for her phone.

Olivia was so sick of trying to figure things out. She felt like she could sleep for a week. Resting her head back on her knees, she whispered a silent hope.

Don't die, Luke. Don't die.

20

Olivia and Ynes entered the hospital and found out that Luke was alive and in surgery and that he would survive his injuries. Both young women breathed sighs of relief.

Ynes was exhausted and decided to head back to her apartment. She was leaving the next day to attend a conference in New York City and she needed to pack and get things ready to go. Olivia wanted to stay at the hospital for a while hoping to see Luke once he was moved to recovery so she was directed to a waiting room where she could sit until Luke's surgery was completed.

Olivia entered the empty, dimly lit waiting room and went to take a seat when she noticed someone slumped in a chair, asleep. The person's jacket covered most of her face, but her short blonde hair was shining in the moonlight that filtered in through the window glass.

"Kayla," Olivia spoke quietly. She touched her shoulder.

Kayla bolted up, blinking, trying to orient herself to her surroundings. "Oh. Olivia." She rubbed her eyes.

Olivia took off her coat and draped it over the arm of one of the chairs. She collapsed into the seat next to Kayla. "I didn't think you'd be waiting."

Kayla stretched and leaned back. "Yeah, well, I wanted to see how Luke was doing." She sat up straight and faced Olivia. Dark circles tinged the skin under her eyes. "I didn't stab him. I swear. I found him like that. I didn't do it."

Olivia nodded. Kayla seemed sincere in her denial, but Olivia just didn't know what to believe anymore. "Who's doing this?" she muttered.

"I don't know. It's horrible. Who would want them killed? What's the reason?" Kayla ran her long, slender fingers through her bangs. Her spiked up hair had relaxed and now hung over her forehead giving her a soft, almost elf-like appearance. "They never got to live their lives." She looked at Olivia, her face lined with worry. "Will the police arrest me? My prints are on the knife. How will they ever believe I didn't stab Luke?"

"I don't know. You'll get a lawyer. The truth will come out. You'll be okay."

Kayla whispered, "Will I?" Her shoulders slumped.

"Was Luke conscious when you found him?" Olivia asked.

Kayla stared at the floor. "No. He was on the floor. I thought he was dead."

"I wonder if he got a look at his attacker. The police will question him. He's the only one who has survived an attack." Olivia speculated, "It must be the same person who killed the others. Maybe the knife can be tied back to Christian and Gary … and, Jack."

Kayla massaged the back of her neck. "Luke must have fought back. His hands...they were all cut up." She winced recalling the image of Luke's bloody hands.

Olivia nodded. "Maybe the attacker heard you come in and took off. Maybe you saved him."

Kayla's eyes were wide at the thought she may have interrupted the attack. A buzz from her pocket indicated an incoming text message and she reached in and took out her phone. "It's Eric. He wants to know how Luke is doing. He's on his way to keep me company. He's just outside."

"What time is it?"

"Two am."

"He's quite a friend to come here so late."

"Yeah. He's good to me. He comes to most of my gigs, makes sure I get home safe." Kayla's fingers flew over the screen of her phone sending a reply text back to Eric.

"How'd you meet?" Olivia shifted in the chair trying to find a more comfortable position.

"At the coffee shop. We've both been working there for a couple of years."

"He told us he graduated from MIT and worked at a start-up for a while."

"Yeah, he's wicked smart. He knows everything about computers, online security, all that stuff."

"He got laid off?" Olivia asked. She wanted to see if Kayla knew that Eric had been fired from his position at LearnApp.

"He didn't care about getting laid off. He's working on his own project."

"What is it that he's working on?"

Kayla pulled a few dollars from her jeans. "I have no idea. I don't understand software or hardware or whatever he's doing. You want a coffee from the machine?"

"No, thanks."

Kayla got up and went to the vending machine, fed in her dollar bills, punched in some numbers, and returned with a paper cup of steaming coffee.

"What's Eric's last name?" Olivia asked.

"Daniels."

"Huh," Olivia said. "That's weird."

"What?"

"I met a guy the other night. He said he had worked

with an Eric Daniels at a start-up in Kendall. LearnApp"

"Yeah, that's where Eric worked. What's weird then?" Kayla sipped her coffee.

"The guy said this Eric he knew got fired because he lost his temper all the time. He couldn't get along with anyone. One day, he ranted about a co-worker to the CEO and security had to escort him out."

"That can't be the Eric I know." Kayla smiled. "Eric's not like that."

"Eric's not like what?" A man's voice asked.

Olivia's head whipped around. Eric was standing in the doorway of the waiting room. Kayla looked up, her eyes bright when she saw him there. "Hey. You got here fast." She stood and went over to hug him.

As Eric patted Kayla's back, he gave Olivia a cold stare that sent a chill along her spine.

Olivia assumed Eric had overheard the things she was telling Kayla and she wanted to deflect Eric's attention away from her. She stood up. "Time for a bathroom break."

"I'll go with you." Kayla handed her coffee cup to Eric. "Be right back."

The two young women walked down the corridor looking for the restroom.

Olivia didn't like the way Eric always seemed to be hanging around Kayla, like she needed a bodyguard.

Kayla didn't know that Eric got fired from his job. He must have wanted to save face in front of her. Olivia wondered if the guy who said he'd worked with Eric was exaggerating about Eric's behavior. Did Eric get fired or did he really get laid off? Olivia asked, "Does Eric live in Cambridge?"

"Yeah, off Mass Ave somewhere."

"You've never been to his place?"

"No. That's funny, huh? I never realized that. We always go out somewhere."

"You two hang out a lot?"

"Yeah. After work we might go for a drink, to the movies. We spend a lot of time together. He's like my brother."

"He doesn't look at you like he's your brother," Olivia said.

Kayla let out a chuckle. "What do you mean? It's not like that. Not at all."

Olivia wasn't so sure about that. She had the distinct impression that Eric didn't think of Kayla as a sister. "Well, he sure doesn't like me."

"Oh, he's just protective of me. Don't let him bother you."

They found the bathroom and then returned to the waiting room. Eric was sitting slouched in one of the chairs staring at his phone.

Olivia didn't like the vibe Eric was giving off, so she picked up her coat and put it on. "I think I'll head home. Melissa went home sick earlier and I'd like to check on her. Maybe I can call the hospital in the morning and find out how Luke is doing."

"I'll text you," Kayla said, "when he gets out of surgery and after I speak with the nurse or the doctor. I can give you an update. Give me your number. I'll give you mine." Kayla took out her phone.

Olivia reached into her coat pocket. It was empty. She stuck her hands in the other pockets searching for her phone. "Where's my phone? Oh, no, I hope it's not lost. I just got it fixed."

Eric bent and reached under the chair next to him. "This it?" He held it out to Olivia. His expression still looked angry ... or cold. Olivia couldn't read it.

"Yeah, thanks. That's it. It must have fallen out of my pocket when I took off my coat."

She and Kayla exchanged numbers.

"I'll let you know as soon as I hear anything," Kayla said.

"Thanks. I'll see you later." Olivia couldn't get out of the room fast enough. *Why is Eric so damn antagonistic towards me?* She headed out of the hospital entrance and hailed a cab. She gave her address and leaned her head against the back seat. Her eyes nearly slammed shut and she had to fight to keep them open during the drive to her apartment. All Olivia wanted was to crawl into her bed and fall asleep.

21

Olivia entered the apartment and looked in on Melissa. Her friend was sleeping soundly and, not wanting to wake her, she went to her own room, stripped her clothes off, and let them drop on the floor. She pulled on her pajamas, climbed under the covers, and was asleep seconds after her head hit the pillow.

It seemed like she'd slept for only a few minutes when she heard Melissa in the bathroom. Light was streaming in through the window. Olivia checked the clock on her night stand. Ten in the morning.

"Liv? You awake?' Melissa came into the room and sat on Olivia's bed. She had dark circles under her eyes and her hair was matted on her head from fever.

Olivia sat up. "You okay? How do you feel?"

"Wiped. I went to bed as soon as I came home last

night. What time did you get back? Did you find Luke?"

Olivia had forgotten that Melissa didn't know anything about the events of last night. "It's a long story. Are you up for it?"

Melissa stretched out on the bed next to Olivia and put her head on the pillow. "Maybe. Tell me what happened."

"Wait." Olivia reached for her phone and checked for messages. Kayla had sent a text a few hours ago saying Luke was out of surgery and that he would be in the hospital for about four days. He would be okay. Olivia breathed another sigh of relief.

"What's up?" Melissa asked.

"A lot." Olivia proceeded to relay what had happened from the time she left Melissa outside the club until she finally returned home in the early morning hours.

Melissa propped her head up with her hand. "I thought it was over. I thought it was probably that stupid football player, Adam Johnson, who killed the guys. It must have been a nightmare to find Luke like that. Thank heavens he'll be all right."

"It was surreal. I couldn't believe it happened again. I was so hopeful that Adam Johnson was the killer. My heart almost stopped when I saw Kayla next to Luke holding a knife. I was terrified," Olivia said. "I thought she stabbed him. I thought she would attack us. I wasn't sure what to do."

"You were brave not to run away."

"I'm not brave. I just knew we had to help Luke, and anyway, Ynes was with me. I started babbling at Kayla, asking her questions. Turns out, I believe her answers, but Ynes thinks Kayla is guilty."

"Will the police ever figure this out? Are they going to find the killer or is it just going to go on and on?"

"How many guys will be attacked before it stops?" Olivia asked. "I'm feeling low, Mel. Sort of hopeless. Why can't this...this evil, be stopped?"

Melissa's eyes closed, as she mumbled, "The eternal optimist isn't allowed to lose hope."

Olivia pulled the blanket up around her shoulders. "I feel like the bad guys keep winning. How can we stop them?"

Melissa was drifting off to sleep. "Don't give up, Liv."

Olivia pressed her hand against Melissa's cheek. "Your fever is back. Did you take anything when you got up?"

Melissa didn't answer. Her breathing indicated she'd fallen into a deep sleep. Olivia adjusted the blanket over Melissa and then slid out of the bed. She needed a shower and some breakfast before she headed off to her tutoring session, but she hoped a short run would lift her spirits and clear her head.

OLIVIA STARTED JOGGING down her street when a text message arrived to let her know that her tutoring pupil wouldn't be in today so the session was cancelled. Since her day was now free of obligations, she decided to take advantage of the time and do a long run. She headed in the direction of Cambridge so that she could jog along the Charles River. The sun sparkled in the gorgeous blue sky and even though the day was cold, she knew her inner temperature would adjust and she'd be comfortable once she had been moving for a while.

Images of Christian and Gary and Luke popped into Olivia's head and she tried to brush them away by focusing her thoughts on other things. She pictured her home in Ogunquit, the beach, the rocky cliffs at the ocean's edge, and summer days spent swimming and kayaking.

When she reached Harvard Square, Olivia turned right onto JFK Street and jogged to Memorial Drive and the grassy area that lined the river. Her lungs ached from the chilly air and her muscles burned from her recent lack of exercise so she slowed to a brisk walk and followed the path along the water.

As she walked along, her thoughts drifted to Kayla and her unrequited love for Christian and it tugged at Olivia's heart.

Her phone buzzed again and Olivia removed it to read the text. It was from Jason, the guy she'd met at the formal dance. She sighed at his request to get together and then pushed the phone back in her pocket. Jason had first contacted Olivia several days ago, and she nicely, but firmly explained that it wasn't a good time for her to start a relationship. Since then, Jason had sent her a bouquet of flowers and numerous texts asking her to meet up.

Olivia replied to Jason's first messages, telling him he was a nice guy, but that she couldn't get involved. She'd been ignoring his more recent texts and wondering when Jason would finally stop nagging at her. Walking around alone at night, she always looked over her shoulder worried that Jason might pop up somewhere.

A prickle of apprehension skittered through her body and after a few moments, the sensation gave way to annoyance. Olivia was angry and bothered that Jason couldn't let go of the idea of getting together and she was annoyed with herself for feeling on edge and vulnerable. His unwanted attention gave her the feeling that he was stalking her. She started jogging again trying to shake off her negative emotions and she trained her focus on the scenery and the people around her.

The river reflected the blue of the sky, couples walked hand and hand along the riverbank, parents pushed strollers, and some guys tossed a football around on the grass.

The football reminded her of Ynes' friend Eva and the illegal activities of Adam Johnson. Selling drugs out of the gym, threatening Gary, stalking Eva. Disgust flooded Olivia's body as she thought about people's desires and the actions some took when they couldn't get what they wanted from someone.

An idea formed in Olivia's mind and the surprise of it caused her to stop short on the jogging path. She wondered why she hadn't thought of it before. The runner behind her almost collided into her back.

"Sorry!" she called as the runner side-stepped her and ran past.

Olivia took off running up a side street and turned right onto Mass Ave moving as quickly as she could, heading to Kendall Square. *Why didn't I ask this before?*

A BLOCK from the Cream and Roses Cafe, Olivia slowed to a walk to bring her breathing back to normal. Up ahead, she caught sight of a blonde with short hair bobbing amongst the crowd of people on the sidewalk.

Olivia quickened her pace to catch up and called out, "Kayla!"

Kayla turned, surprised to see Olivia. "Hey. What are you doing here?"

They walked side by side.

"I was out for a jog. I needed a long run after last night."

"A long jog wouldn't be my first choice after a night like last night. Thankfully, Luke will recover."

"You're working now?"

"Yeah. I thought about calling in sick. I only slept a few hours after getting home from the hospital, but I need the money."

Olivia asked, "Do you have a minute before you go in?" They were standing in front of the café.

"Um, I guess. I need to go in soon. I really only have a minute. What's up?" Her blue eyes stared at Olivia.

"I was thinking." Olivia shuffled her feet and looked down at the sidewalk for a second trying to think of how to word things properly. She looked back at Kayla.

"What is it?" Kayla asked, her eyes narrowed.

"Did Eric know you were going to Christian's party the night of the murders?"

"Yeah. Why?"

"What was he doing that night?"

It dawned on Kayla what Olivia might be hinting at and her lips tightened. "What are you thinking?"

"I'm just wondering if..."

Kayla's eyes narrowed and she cut Olivia off. "Are

you accusing Eric of the murders? Really? How could you think that? Why would you think that?" Kayla's voice got louder and passers-by shot her a look.

Kayla whirled away from Olivia and took a step towards the café's entrance.

"Kayla. Wait."

Kayla stopped and turned back to Olivia, moving in close. She kept her voice low. "How did you come up with this ridiculous idea? Just because Eric doesn't like you and Melissa?"

"No. I didn't say I think he's the killer. I'm just wondering where he was that night. He's so protective of you. I wondered if he tailed you to Christian's to be sure you'd be okay. You must have told him that you hadn't been invited to the party. He was probably worried how things would go. I thought maybe he might have hung around outside to be sure you didn't leave upset."

Kayla's body relaxed as her anger started to dissipate.

Olivia went on, "If he was there, outside, I thought you could ask him if he saw anything unusual. Maybe if he thinks back on it, something, somebody, might stand out. Could you ask him if he was there? If he did go there watching out for you, he probably kept it to himself. Maybe he thinks you'd be angry that he followed you there, so he's keeping quiet about it. He could've seen something that might be helpful."

"I guess it's not that wild of an idea," Kayla said. "But he wasn't there. He went to a department party at MIT that night. He wanted to see some friends from out of town who were going to be there."

"Oh." Olivia's shoulders slumped. "Well, it was worth a shot. I'd hoped he was outside. I hoped he'd seen something."

"I have to get in to work." Kayla turned to go in, but said over her shoulder, "Sorry I got upset." She opened the door and disappeared into the busy café.

Olivia shivered from standing out in the cold, covered in sweat. She considered going into the café to warm up before heading home, but decided against it. She didn't know if Eric was inside working and she sure didn't want to see him.

Briskly rubbing her arms and legs to warm them up, she turned to start her jog back to Somerville, cursing herself for not bringing along some cash or her subway card.

22

Olivia carried a gift bag filled with homemade cookies and some fancy chocolates as she walked down the hospital corridor looking for Luke's room. When she found the number she wanted, she hesitated, a bit nervous about seeing Luke and talking about what happened to him. She took a deep breath, put a smile on her face, and entered the room.

"Hey," she said.

Luke was lying in the hospital bed, the head of the frame elevated so that he was almost in a sitting position. Bandages were visible at his neck and on his hands, and Olivia's breath caught in her throat remembering Luke prone in the hallway of his building covered in blood.

"Hey," Luke said. His voice was strong and he had

good color in his face. He smiled at Olivia, his eyes bright.

Olivia gave him a gentle hug.

"I'm okay," he chuckled. "You won't break me."

Olivia's eyes misted over and she touched his hand. "I'm so glad you're okay." She blinked to clear the emotion from her eyes. "I baked you some cookies and there are chocolates, too." She handed him the gift bag. "Melissa would have come, but she has the flu."

A young man with dark brown eyes and sandy blonde hair sat on the opposite side of Luke's bed. He cleared his throat. "Are you going to introduce me?" he teased his friend.

"Olivia, this is my friend, Rob. We know each other from MIT. Rob, this is Olivia, my hero."

Olivia shook her head and blushed. "No, I'm not." Rob and Olivia shook hands across Luke's bed, and then she sat down in the chair that was pulled close to the head of the bed.

"I heard all about your heroics." Rob smiled.

"Hardly. Our friend, Ynes, was there, too. And, Kayla. Everyone played a part in helping." Olivia looked at Luke. "You are one tough guy. You're the one who survived the attack."

"Must be my solid musculature," Luke joked, and then his face turned serious. "Thank you. You saved my life."

Olivia shook her head. "I think Kayla is the one to

thank. I think she must have interrupted the attack. We just called '911.'"

Luke said, "Rob and I were just talking about how I could have avoided all this. I was supposed to go to the MIT department party with him the night Christian and Gary were killed."

"Yeah," Rob said. "But he bailed on me to go to Christian's. Guess he learned his lesson never to bail on me."

Olivia smiled. She liked the easy banter between the guys and thought it was probably just what Luke needed to lift his spirits. "Kayla's Eric was at that party. He should have taken Kayla to it, then she would have avoided the mess of that night, too."

"Eric, the rude weasel?" Luke asked.

Olivia smiled. "Yeah, him."

"Who's this?" Rob asked.

"Eric Daniels," Olivia told him. "He graduated last year."

Rob said, "I know who he is. I didn't see him at the party. He wasn't a very social guy. Never took part in anything the department put on."

"That's because he's a rude weasel." Luke turned to Olivia. "Can I eat one of the cookies you brought?" The bandages on Luke's hands made it awkward for him to unwrap the package so Olivia reached for the bag and opened it so that Luke could get at the treats.

He chewed. "Delicious." Glancing at Rob, he said,

"Too bad you weren't attacked. You might have gotten some home baked cookies."

"Maybe I'll just help myself." Rob moved to get up from his seat.

"Will you give one to him, Olivia? Otherwise, he'll get cranky."

They chuckled and she offered Rob a cookie.

Olivia hated to bring it up, but she needed to ask. "Luke, did you see the attacker?"

The mirth left Luke's face and for a moment, his eyes clouded over as he looked across the room at nothing. His voice was soft. "There was a knock on my door. I thought it was Kayla. We were going to meet you and Melissa at the club." He stopped, and then gathered himself to continue. "It was quick. He lunged at me. I was so shocked, the knife wounds barely registered. I fought back, but he was like a maniac. I don't even remember going down."

"What did he look like?" Olivia asked.

Luke turned to her. "I couldn't see his face."

Olivia waited.

"It was the black ski mask again. He was dressed in black. He was wearing gloves."

"Was he big?"

Luke shook his head. "My height, slim." He rested his head back on the pillow. "Funny, it could even have been a woman, I suppose."

Olivia's eyes narrowed, surprised that Luke

suggested that the killer could be a woman. "Why do you say that?"

"I don't know." His face looked thoughtful. "I guess it wasn't."

Olivia asked, "The police questioned you?"

Luke nodded.

Olivia wanted to say something hopeful. "At least they have the knife as evidence. Maybe it will give them some clues."

The three sat quietly for a minute, and then Rob said, "Let's talk about something important. Like whether or not I can have another one of those cookies."

Chuckling, Olivia passed Rob another cookie, handed Luke a second one, and then chatted for another forty-five minutes before a nurse came in and shooed them out so that Luke could rest.

WHEN OLIVIA GOT HOME, Melissa was snuggled under a blanket resting on the sofa with her head on a pillow. Olivia made her toast and tea and pulled the coffee table closer to the couch so that Melissa would be able to easily reach the plate and her drink. Olivia sat across from her on the other sofa.

"I can't shake this stupid fever," Melissa mumbled.

"It hasn't even been forty-eight hours." Olivia

pulled her legs up onto the sofa. "Would you like a cool cloth for your forehead?"

"Yes, please."

Olivia went into the bathroom and put a face cloth under the tap, squeezed it out, and brought it to Melissa and placed it over her forehead. Melissa's eyes were only half open.

"I can't be sick. I have to go to class tomorrow."

"I don't think that's a good idea. Email your lab partner in the afternoon. Ask her for a copy of the notes. I'll meet her and get them for you. You need to rest," Olivia said. "If you try to do too much too soon, it will just take longer to get well."

Olivia's phone buzzed and she read the text. "It's from Ynes. She's on the train to New York heading for a conference. She'll be there for a couple of days. She hopes you feel better. She wants us to send any updates about Luke and any news about the case."

"There won't be any news about the case. They won't ever figure it out," Melissa said from under the cloth covering her face.

Olivia stared at her phone. "Why is this thing losing its charge so fast?"

"Did you charge it recently?" Melissa asked.

"It never used to need charging so often. It's so annoying."

Melissa said, "Bring it to the phone store. Or get a new one. You've had that thing for ages."

"I don't want to go back to the store. I just had the screen replaced from when that stupid Adam Johnson knocked it out of my hand at the gym," Olivia grumped. "Why can't things work properly?" She placed the phone on the side table.

Melissa pushed the facecloth aside, yawned, and closed her eyes.

Olivia said, "You're making me sleepy just looking at you."

"Don't look at me then," she mumbled.

Olivia stretched out on the sofa. "Maybe I'll just close my eyes for a few minutes. I didn't get much sleep last night after getting back so late from the hospital."

She dozed off quickly and she and Melissa napped for two hours.

23

A fter a busy day of classes, Olivia walked down the hill to Davis Square to the phone store. It was nearly six in the evening and the sun had already set shrouding the city in darkness. Olivia wanted to pick up some tea at the convenience store so that Melissa wouldn't run out and she was planning to put together some broth and rice in case Melissa wanted to eat a little. Approaching the phone store, she hoped it wouldn't take long for them to determine why her battery was draining.

Olivia tugged the door open, entered, and found a tech customer service rep to speak with about what could be causing her phone to lose its charge so fast. She really didn't want to have to buy a new one, but her current phone needed almost constant charging now. The tech guy took Olivia to a work table in the rear of the store to take a look at the cell phone.

"It should hold the charge a lot longer than what you're saying is happening. Sometimes apps are running in the background that you're unaware of and that drains the battery."

"I don't have anything different on it than what I've always had," Olivia said.

"Maybe you just need to replace the battery." The guy fiddled with the phone for a few minutes. "Here. There seems to be an app that's running. Yeah, this is it. It's sending out info on your whereabouts. Like a constant GPS signal being transmitted. That's what's doing the draining."

"I don't have an app like that. Why would I need to send out my location constantly?"

The guy tapped on Olivia's phone, his face intent on whatever he was seeing on the screen. "Well, that's what it is. You've got the app downloaded."

"Can you get rid of it?"

"There's a way to disable it, but we're short-handed today. You'll need to leave it here for a couple of hours. One of us can disable it in-between customers. It doesn't take that long, but we should check the phone for anything else that might be contributing to the battery running down."

Olivia scowled. "I can't leave it today. My friend is

sick. I want her to be able to contact me. I'll bring the phone in when she's feeling better."

"Does your friend have some need to track you?"

"What do you mean?"

"It could be that someone downloaded this app to keep track of you."

A chill ran across Olivia's skin. "There are ways to do that? Without my permission?"

The tech guy nodded. "Someone could have gotten at your phone and put the app on there without you knowing."

"Well, heck." Olivia's heartbeat speeded up as she looked at her phone. "But, there's no icon on the screen for the app."

"There are ways to delete the icon so you don't know you're being tracked."

Olivia's eyes were wide. "How long would it take for someone to do that to my phone?"

"Not long. A couple of minutes. Not even."

"How is that even legal?" Olivia rubbed her temple. "How is that possible?" Her mind was racing, trying to imagine who would do this.

"Maybe one of your friend's did it as a joke."

She looked at the tech guy. "It's not funny. I'll try to come back tomorrow. I want this thing off my phone." She dropped the phone into the front pocket of her backpack. "What's the name of the app? In case, you're not here when I come back."

The tech guy said, "Stalker."

The blood drained out of Olivia's head.

Jason, from the formal.

OLIVIA STORMED out of the phone store and tore up College Ave heading for her apartment. She hoped that Melissa was awake and not too groggy so that she could release the rant that was building inside her with every step she took. She was so distracted by the app on her phone that she forgot all about stopping at the grocery store. *How dare he put an app on my phone? How dare he track my movements?* She stopped walking and dug into her backpack for her phone. She decided to send Jason a scathing text blasting him for his actions and invading her privacy. While scrolling through her contacts for Jason's number, a text came in. It was from Kayla.

Can you meet me at the café? It's important. I know something about the case. You need to hear it. Bring Melissa.

Olivia's hands shook with excitement hoping that this might be a break in the case.

Melissa's sick. When should I meet you?

Kayla's reply was almost immediate: *Come now.*

Olivia tossed the phone in her backpack and wheeled around to retrace her steps back to Davis

Square where she could pick up the "T" to take her to the café in Kendall Square.

OLIVIA OPENED the glass door of the Cream and Roses Cafe, looked around at the tables and chairs, and not seeing Kayla, walked up to the counter and ordered a tea.

"Has Kayla been in?" she asked the guy taking orders.

"Kayla? I don't know. I just got here."

"I'm supposed to meet her. I'll wait," Olivia said. She carried her tea to one of the tables near the window so she could look out at the people passing by in the darkness. Possible ideas about the case flashed through her mind. *What does Kayla know? How did she find something out? Will it lead to the killer?*

A woman barista came out of the back room and spoke to the guy working the counter who nodded in Olivia's direction. The woman waved at Olivia to call her over.

"You're looking for Kayla? She was here earlier, but she left. She was with Eric."

"When did she leave?" Olivia asked.

"Oh, I don't know." She glanced up to the wall clock as she added whipped cream to the top of a coffee drink. "Maybe, a little less than an hour ago."

"Did she say where they were headed?"

"I heard them say something about stopping by Eric's place. He wanted to show her something."

"Thanks," Olivia said. "They must be coming back. Kayla asked me to meet her here." She returned to her table and sat sipping her tea. Olivia wondered if Eric had used his computer skills to find out something about the killings. She thought he must want to show Kayla what he'd discovered. She glanced out the window, hoping they would return soon.

Olivia tried browsing the internet on her phone to distract her, but her mind was so antsy waiting to hear Kayla's news that she couldn't concentrate on anything. She put the phone on the table next to her tea cup. Olivia thought over the details of the case attempting to find something that she'd missed. Her fingers drummed the table top absent-mindedly as she wondered what was taking so long for Kayla and Eric to come back.

After a few minutes, she lifted her phone and sent a text to Kayla asking when she would return to the café. Olivia drained her tea. She stared at her phone. No reply from Kayla.

She leaned back in her chair and crossed her ankles under the table, questioning herself as to why she was such an impatient person. Trying some things she'd learned in a yoga class, Olivia relaxed her muscles and slowed her breathing rate.

An alarm buzzed in her brain and she sat up in her chair. At the hospital after the attack on Luke, Kayla had told Olivia that she had never been to Eric's apartment.

Why would he ask her to go there tonight?

Her heart rate increased and she stood up so fast that her chair almost tipped over. She approached the counter to speak to the barista again.

"You said Kayla and Eric were headed to his place?"

The barista nodded and reached for a cup.

Olivia asked the barista another question. "I was wondering if there was a way to find out if Eric was working a certain night. A couple of weeks ago." Olivia persisted. "It was a Saturday night, October 12. Is there any way somebody could check to see who worked that night?" Olivia remembered that Luke's friend Rob mentioned that he didn't see Eric at the MIT party the night that Christian and Luke were killed. *Maybe Eric came into work that night?*

The woman gave Olivia an annoyed stare, and then she rolled her eyes and glanced at the guy working the register. "Harry. Will you go look at the shift schedule? Find out who was working the night of October 12." She snapped a plastic cover over a drink cup and slid it onto the counter. Harry went into the back room.

"Thanks," Olivia said as she checked her phone again. Still no answer from Kayla.

A few minutes later, Harry came out. "It was Josie and Karen." He took up his post at the register.

The barista lifted her eyes to Olivia to be sure she had heard what Harry said.

"So Eric wasn't working that night?" Olivia asked.

"Guess not."

"Could the schedule be wrong?"

"No. That's how they calculate the payroll for the week. Everyone's careful to log any changes."

"Thanks." Olivia went back to her table with her mind racing.

Eric says he went to the MIT department party that night. Luke's friend said that he didn't remember seeing Eric there. He said he didn't remember Eric ever going to any department events. Did Eric follow Kayla to Christian and Gary's? Why did he take Kayla to his place tonight?

Olivia stared off into space. A cold chill trickled from the back of her throat down into her stomach. *Could they…? Oh, no.*

Olivia bolted from her seat and approached the barista again. "Can you tell me Eric's address?"

The barista's brow furrowed and she gave Olivia a look that could kill. Before she could reply, Olivia lied, "Eric asked me to come to his house tonight. He said it was important. I lost his address and he isn't answering his phone. It must be dead."

"Why don't you try Kayla? They left together."

"I did. She hasn't answered me."

The cash register guy was listening.

Olivia smiled at him. "It's kind of important."

The guy left the cash register and returned to the back room for a second time. He came out with a piece of paper in his hand. He gave it to Olivia. "We're not supposed to give out addresses, but its only Eric. Don't tell anyone I gave it to you."

"Thanks. I really appreciate it." Olivia wanted to hug the guy. She read the address, and as she exited the café, she pulled up a map of Cambridge on her phone.

She hurried along the dark sidewalk, dodging around people who were heading out for the night. Olivia broke into a jog.

Turning off Mass Ave onto a side street, Olivia tried calling Kayla as she ran, but no one picked up. A wave of anxiety washed through her veins. A gust of wind whipped Olivia's hair into her eyes and she shivered, but she was sure it wasn't the breeze that was chilling her.

She sprinted for a few more blocks, headed down another side street, and searched the numbers on the buildings as she passed. She halted in front of Eric's apartment building and stood on the sidewalk staring at it. Blood pounded in her head. She couldn't ignore the warning signals her body was sending her.

Sometimes deep in your heart you know something, you've probably known it all along, but your mind just doesn't process it.

Olivia's brain buzzed. She couldn't deny it.

She knew who killed Christian. And Gary. And Jack.

24

Olivia sucked in a breath and hurried up the stone steps to the landing of Eric's building. She scanned the intercom buttons for Eric's name and pushed the corresponding button to announce her arrival. She stood shivering on the landing, waiting.

"Yes?" A male voice questioned over the intercom.

"I'm a friend of Eric and Kayla's. Can I come up?"

The door buzzed and Olivia opened it and entered the building. She walked up the stairs to the second floor landing, found the right number, and knocked. A young guy in a flannel shirt opened the door.

He said, "I don't think they're here anymore. I heard them talking earlier. I think they left."

Olivia's heart sank. "Oh."

"The intercom is broken. I can hear you, but it

doesn't transmit from up here down to the lobby. That's why I buzzed you in."

"Thanks," Olivia said. She had an idea. "Can I knock on Eric's door? Maybe they're watching a movie or something? They said they would leave something of mine in his room," she lied. "Could I just check it out?"

"He usually keeps his door locked, but you can see if they're in there or if they left it open for you."

"Why does he keep his bedroom door locked? Doesn't he trust you?" She smiled to make the guy think she was joking.

"Actually, I don't think he does," Eric's roommate said. "I never gave him cause not to trust me, but Eric's kind of quirky. He's quiet, neat in the common areas, but he seems a little paranoid. Stays to himself a lot. I don't have much interaction with him."

Olivia followed the roommate down the hallway to Eric's bedroom.

"This is his." He knocked. It was quiet. He tried the door to see if it was unlocked. It didn't budge. "Guess he locked it when they left. No surprise."

"Do you have a key? I really need to pick up my thing."

The roommate chuckled. "Eric wouldn't give anyone a key."

"Oh," Olivia said. She had to get into the bedroom. "Are there any extra apartment keys lying around? I wonder if there's a duplicate for Eric's room."

"There are some keys in the kitchen cabinet. I don't know what they open though."

Olivia was impatient. "Could we try them?" She needed to get rid of the roommate for a minute.

"I'll get them," the roommate said.

"Thanks."

When he disappeared down the hall, Olivia pulled out her credit card, and with trembling fingers, slid it in the crack of the door and jiggled it slightly. She heard the lock pop. During his many renovations, Olivia's neighbor and father figure, Joe, had learned a good deal about locks and how they worked. When Olivia was in middle school, Joe taught her about locking systems and how to open a simple one with a credit card. You never knew when skills could come in handy. Olivia's Aunt Aggie was none too pleased with Joe for teaching a twelve-year-old how to pick a lock.

Thank you, Joe.

"It's open," Olivia called to the roommate.

He came down the hall holding the extra keys. "It seemed locked when I tried it."

"I jiggled it. It must have been stuck," Olivia offered. She turned the knob and pushed the door open. The roommate stepped into the dark room ahead of her and flicked the wall switch.

"What the...?" he muttered. "What the hell?"

Olivia pushed into the room behind the roommate to see what he was commenting on. Her eyes went wide and her heart skipped a beat as she pivoted taking in the strange sight.

Every available piece of wall space was covered with photographs. It was the same photograph, over and over. Each one of them was of Kayla... with Christian.

"Oh, no," Olivia whispered. "No." The strangeness of the display nearly choked her. She turned in a slow circle taking it all in.

The blinds were pulled down over the windows. One small dresser stood up against the wall space between the two windows. All the drawers were half open with clothes spilling over the tops. A mattress was near the far wall, on the floor, a sheet and a thin blanket crumpled on top of it. A musty, stale smell permeated the space.

"Kayla was here tonight?" Olivia could barely get the words out. "She saw this?"

"Yeah. At least I thought so. I didn't see them. I was in the kitchen. I just heard Eric talking and a woman's voice. They were in here." The guy stood dumbfounded in the center of the room.

The apartment smoke alarm shrieked. Olivia jumped.

"My food's burning!" The roommate ran from the room.

Olivia turned to look at a long table that ran almost the length of one wall. Eric was using it as a desk and had computer equipment and displays covering most of the space. Some of the displays were on and one was showing a map of Cambridge. A small green dot was blinking. Olivia leaned close. The dot was located on the map on Eric's street, over Eric's building. Above the dot, was an "O."

Olivia's stomach felt like it was filling with ice water and her temples pulsed like they were about to explode. She ripped her phone from her pocket and stared at it. She lifted her eyes to the computer display. "Monster," she whispered, "you've been tracking me."

Fury rose in her chest and she balled her hand into a fist. Swinging her arm up and then forward, she punched the display sending it crashing against the wall.

Olivia's chest rose and fell, her breath coming in gasps, in and out, in and out, as rage consumed her. "He's been tracking me!" she roared. She glared at the phone in her hand and was about to smash it against the desk when it buzzed with a text from Kayla's number.

Guess who this is? Hint: it's not Kayla. Get home. Do not call the police. Keep the phone with you so I know you aren't making any stops for help. Don't speak to anyone. There's a cab outside. Take it home. I'm timing you. Follow these instructions or they're both dead.

Olivia's stomach roiled. The hand holding her phone dropped limply to her side as her eyes shifted to the wall in a haze. There was a cork board on the wall above Eric's table. A push pin was stabbed through the middle of a picture holding it in the center of the bulletin board.

It was a picture of Kayla with Luke.

Olivia's vision blurred. She placed her hands on the desk to keep from toppling over. Her right hand touched something. She shifted her gaze to it. A black ski mask was on the desk.

25

Olivia raced up the stairs, two at a time, to her sixth floor apartment. The exertion of climbing six flights in a state of anxiety and fear made her lungs burn. Her terror nearly gagged her.

She was about to jab the key in the lock, but stopped, realizing that she had to compose herself before facing whatever Eric had in store. She needed her wits about her if she and Melissa and Kayla were going to emerge from this confrontation alive.

Olivia moved away from her apartment door, leaned against the wall, and focused on breathing in through her nose and out through her mouth. She had to be ready for whatever Eric was going to throw at her.

She needed to take all of the tension and fear flowing through her veins and concentrate it into energy that she could use against him. Straightening her shoulders, she turned back to her door. She had to help her friends.

Olivia abruptly halted. *How would Eric know if I called the police? Damn.* She mentally berated herself for being so stupid. She pulled out her phone to make the call and then hesitated. *But would he know? Does he have something on this phone that monitors my calls and texts? Is that even possible? What if I call the police and Eric knows I did it? He'll kill Melissa and Kayla.* Her heart sank. She couldn't take the chance.

Even though she knew that Eric was tracking her, Olivia inserted her key into the lock as quietly as she could. She pressed her hand against the door to open it.

Her auditory system was on high alert. The living room was dark, the few furniture pieces draped in menacing shadow. She wouldn't chance flicking on the overhead light. Her heartbeat thudded in her ears.

Olivia shifted her feet two steps into the room trying to remember which parts of the wood floor always squeaked. She slid her feet, slowly, inch by inch, over the floor, heading for the hall. She stopped.

The tiny blond hairs on her arms stood up. She stood at the edge of the living room, at the corner of the wall. Her eyes had adjusted to the darkness so she held her breath and leaned her head forward just a tiny bit in order to peer down the hallway. Olivia edged forward, shuffled several short steps, and moved into the small kitchen.

She heard a groan come from Melissa's room. Her blood froze and her body shook as she gripped the counter with both hands trying to collect herself. Tears welled in her eyes. Her body felt like it was floating, her senses buzzing. Olivia was afraid she was about to pass out.

She looked at the wall in front of her. The knife rack.

Lifting her hand, she removed the smallest knife. A boning knife. The handle fit well in the palm of her hand. The blade was small, only two inches long at most, but it was sharp. And sharp was what she needed.

Olivia turned back into the hallway. She moved her feet, *quiet, quiet,* while clutching the handle of the knife in her sweaty hand so that the blade pointed behind her.

She paused at Melissa's bedroom door for just a moment, steeling herself to what she might find inside.

"Hello, Olivia." Eric's voice spoke from behind the wooden door.

Olivia sucked in a deep breath, grabbed the knob and flung the door open with such force that it thunked against the bedroom wall.

The overhead light flashed bright in her eyes, blinding her for a half second. When she saw what was in the room, something between a gasp and a sob caught in her throat.

∿

ERIC SAT in Melissa's chair. He had pulled it away from the desk and positioned it in the middle of the room close to the bed. His left hand dangled behind his back. His right hand was bloody. A knife with a long serrated blade was stuck between his legs into the wooden seat of the chair. His lips turned up in a grin.

Kayla sat on the floor between the bed and the chair. She was gagged and her hands and feet were bound. Patches of blood showed on her shirt where Olivia could see the fabric had slices in it. Her forehead had a wide gash and blood ran down the side of her face. Rage flashed in Kayla's eyes.

Melissa was on her back, unconscious, on the bed, her hands and feet bound by heavy rope that tightened around her neck. Streaks of blood stained the pale skin of her arms and face. Olivia knew she was alive because she could make out the slight rising and falling of her chest.

Olivia's stomach clenched and her vision swam. Her fingers squeezed around the handle of the knife she was holding. She wanted to plunge it into Eric's heart.

"Took you long enough," Eric sneered. "I thought

they might both be dead by the time you got here. Now I have the three meddling witches in one room."

Olivia took a step into the bedroom, her eyes blazing. "Monster." She moved two steps towards Kayla.

"Stand right there. Don't you move." Eric's voice was hard, and then it turned taunting. He leaned back in the chair. He nodded his head towards Kayla and kicked her in the back. Olivia winced. "This stupid woman is nothing but trouble," he said. "Just like you."

"What do you want, Eric? What the hell is wrong with you?" Olivia asked. "She's supposed to be your friend."

"I didn't want a friend, Olivia. I loved her. But, I was always just the friend." Eric's eyes narrowed. His face muscles tightened. He tipped his head towards Kayla. "Christian was never good to you. He deserved to die."

Eric looked back at Olivia. "But even with that scum bag out of the picture, I wasn't right for her. She doesn't want me. Now she wants Luke. That coward. I only wanted to make her happy. I *am* going to make her happy. She can go join her dear, sweet Christian. I won't stop her. I'll help her."

"This isn't how you treat people you love." Olivia tried to stall for time to figure out what she could do.

"Loved," Eric said. "Past tense."

"Lots of people get rejected in love, Eric. You aren't the first one it's happened to."

"Oh, shut up, Olivia. Spare me."

Olivia took another step forward. "What I can't understand is why you would try to pin the murders on Kayla. You knew she was going to Christian's Halloween party that night. You knew what she was wearing. All black, the ski mask. So you wore the same thing. And you must be the anonymous caller who told the police that Kayla was at Christian's the night he was killed. You even told us that she was arrested for assault. You made sure everything was pointing at Kayla."

Kayla looked at Eric out of the corner of her eye.

"I thought you were smart, Olivia. You need an explanation?" He snorted. "If the cops suspected her, if she was in trouble, wouldn't she go to her dear friend Eric for comfort? Wouldn't she come to me to help her? Wouldn't she see that I was the one who loved her? The cops might have arrested her, but they never would have been able to build a case against her. I got rid of her love interest and set things up so suspicion would fall on her. Accused and alone, she was supposed to run to me." Eric's face hardened. He glanced at Kayla, his eyes full of hate. "But that didn't happen, did it? She preferred the company of the coward."

Adrenaline pumped through Olivia's body. "Trying to get Kayla arrested for murder is a strange way of showing your love for her."

"Shut up." Eric's eyes narrowed. "I would have liked

to have seen your face when you found the ski mask on your door. Did it scare you?"

"You're a freak," Olivia said.

"Toss me your cell phone," Eric ordered.

Olivia's blood boiled. She pulled the phone from her pocket. Her arm jerked up and she whipped the phone at Eric's head. He ducked, reached out his hand and caught it. He gave Olivia a warning look as he placed the phone in his pocket.

"No calls for help from you." He smiled and then his lips tightened into an angry line.

"Did you have fun tracking me around the city, you psycho?"

Color rose in Eric's face.

Melissa let out a soft moan.

Olivia flicked her eyes to her. "Mel."

"Your pathetic friend can't hear you. I gave her a little something. Something I concocted myself." Eric brought his left hand around to the front. He was holding a syringe and his eyes glinted with delight when he looked up at Olivia.

"She better stay alive." Olivia's left hand clenched into a ball while her right hand tightened around the knife that she held out of Eric's view.

"Or, what?" Eric snorted. He lifted the syringe and turned to Kayla. "Kayla's turn for a little injection."

Kayla shrunk away from him.

Fury exploded in Olivia's veins and she flung

herself at Eric with such force that he toppled over in the chair with Olivia falling on top of him. The syringe dropped from his hand. Kayla scooted away from them on her butt and tried to stand.

Olivia slashed at Eric's arms and upper chest with the boning knife. Eric shrieked and fought Olivia for the weapon. As they tussled for it, the knife fell, clattered across the floor, and slid under the bed.

Eric put his hands around Olivia's neck and tightened, his eyes savage. Olivia grabbed at his hands. She tried to knee him, but he was on top of her now and she couldn't get enough leverage to do any damage. She scratched wildly towards his face with her fingers, but he pushed hard on her neck and fully extended his arms so that his head was just out of her reach.

Olivia gagged. Her eyes bugged.

Kayla's hands were bound by a length of rope to her feet which hampered her ability to get up. She rolled onto her side and used her elbow to give her body the push it needed to hobble up. The rope was too short to allow Kayla to fully stand. She hunched over, her hands close to her feet. Hopping and shuffling, she crossed closer to the fight.

With one hand, Eric grabbed handfuls of Olivia's hair, lifted her head and smashed it onto the floor. Again and again, he pounded her head. Olivia's vision was sparkling, darkness flirting at the edges of her sight.

Like a wild woman, Olivia smashed her fist into Eric's neck trying to crush his Adam's apple. The searing pain halted Eric's attack on her long enough for Olivia to scramble out from under him and crawl a few feet to where the boning knife lay just under the bed.

Eric grabbed her legs and pulled her away from the bed as she was about to grab the knife. She yanked kicked her legs trying to loosen them from his grip.

One foot came free from his hold. Olivia kicked with force into his shin making him bend at the waist. She took advantage of the moment to roll her body into his legs, toppling him. They both tried to scramble to standing position.

Kayla hurtled her body on top of Eric while Olivia crawled under the bed and grasped the knife.

Eric untangled himself from Kayla and scurried across the floor on his hands and knees to the bedroom door, gasping. He stood and whirled, his chest and arms cut and bloody.

Panting, Olivia struggled to her feet holding the knife and she hauled herself into the middle of the room to protect her injured friends. She lowered her chin to level her eyes at Eric. They flashed like a feral animal. While there was breath left in her body, she would not let anything else happen to Melissa or Kayla.

Eric backed out of the room and pulled the bedroom door closed with a fast yank.

Olivia stood in the room, blinking. *What is he up to?* She bent and slashed at Kayla's binds, releasing her.

Kayla pulled the gag off. Olivia knelt and reached for the young woman's shirt to check her injuries.

In between gasps, Kayla said, "It's nothing. Just superficial cuts. He was taunting me. He said he wouldn't kill me until you got here."

Olivia ran to Melissa and touched the side of her neck to check for a pulse. "She's okay." Her eyes filled with tears of relief. "Where's a phone?" Olivia asked. "We'll call for help."

"That bastard took our phones." Kayla rubbed her wrists where the ropes had cut into her skin.

Hearing a sloshing sound in the hallway, Olivia and Kayla pivoted to look at the closed bedroom door. Olivia hurried over and pressed her ear up against it.

The smell of oil or gasoline or lighter fluid flooded her nostrils. She turned the knob and opened the door a crack, clutching the knife tightly in her hand.

The hallway floor was wet.

Eric stood in the living room at the end of the hallway. His arm came up and he threw something towards Olivia. A lighter hit the floor and sent a wall of flames roaring into the air.

Olivia slammed the bedroom door, stumbled back, lost her balance and fell onto her butt, gasping.

The angry flames snarled and cracked at the hallway walls.

"Gasoline. He set the place on fire." Olivia scrambled to her feet.

"That freak." Kayla hurried to the window facing the front of the building and looked out. It was a six story drop to the sidewalk.

"Melissa." Olivia stumbled to the bed and shook her friend's shoulder. Melissa moved a bit, but did not open her eyes. Olivia used her knife to cut the ropes away from her friend's hands, neck, and feet.

"Eric injected Melissa with something," Kayla said, still peering out the front window. "She isn't hurt. The blood is from me. It got on Eric's hands and it got smeared onto Melissa."

Kayla turned away from the window. "There's no fire escape this way." She cursed and rushed to the window that looked out onto the side of the property. The fire escape's metal flooring was broken off and did not reach to Melissa's window. It stopped at the end of the other sixth floor apartment.

Kayla slammed her hand against the wall. "There's no damn fire escape here either. You need to sue the owner of this building."

"I'll put that on my list of things to do." Olivia ran to the bedroom door and placed her palm against it. She yanked her hand back. "It's red hot already. We can't go out this way."

Despair pulled at Olivia's muscles and turned them to rubber. Her panicked eyes flashed about the room. *The window. It's the only way out.* "Bed sheets. Let's pull the sheet off the bed. There must be others in the closet. We'll tie them together and go out the window."

Kayla's mouth dropped open. "You're nuts. Bed sheets won't hold us. And, what about Melissa? How are we going to get her down some bed sheets?"

"Is there a better idea? If there is, let's do it." Olivia stared at Kayla and when she didn't respond with a suggestion, Olivia hurried to the bed and pulled back the blanket. She tugged at the sheet on Melissa's bed, pulling it gently off of her friend.

The air in the bedroom turned hazy as smoke poured under the door. The angry roar of the flames growled at the walls and Olivia wondered how long it would be before they broke into the room.

"A few stupid sheets won't be long enough to tie to the bed and use to climb down to the yard." Kayla's voice shook. Sweat ran down the sides of her face.

"Just tie one end to the leg of the bed. Tight. We are *not* dying here," Olivia muttered as she moved through the haze to the closet and flung open the door. She rustled through the plastic bins on the floor of the closet searching for more sheets, and finding some, dumped the contents of the bin onto the bedroom floor. Reaching for one end of the sheet to start to tie the ends of the clean ones to the one she pulled from Melissa's bed, something on the floor of the closet caught her eye.

Thundering snaps and cracks could be heard in the hall.

"Hurry!" Kayla backed towards the bed, her face white. "Olivia! The flames!

They're breaking through the door!"

Olivia stepped inside the closet and bent to pick something up. She nearly wept with gratitude. *Crazy Melissa.* Olivia smiled and backed out of the closet, turning to show Kayla what she had in her hands.

"What the...?" Kayla gaped.

Olivia stood holding the axe that Melissa had brought back from her visit home.

"Forget the sheets." Olivia kicked the plastic bins out of the way. "We're going to bash through the closet into my room. There are metal rungs attached to the side of the building outside my window."

Kayla didn't need to hear it again. She rushed to the closet and pulled the clothes off the bar that ran the width of the space. "Here. I'll make room for you to get at the wall." She flung the clothes onto the floor of the room. Smoke streamed around and under the bedroom door. Kayla pushed the clothes across the floor, close to, but not touching the space at the bottom of the door to try to stem some of the advancing smoke.

Olivia took the axe and swung it with all her might into the back wall of the closet.

"Pretend it's Eric's face," Kayla shouted to Olivia. "Bash it in!"

A few more swings and Olivia was through the wallboard. Panting, she pushed at it with the end of the axe handle scraping away plaster and board. "We can get through." She backed out of the closet.

Kayla went to the bed to move Melissa. "Come on. We can carry her."

"Here, Kayla. Take the ropes." Olivia bent down to spread one of the sheets on the floor. "We can lie Melissa down on this. Then we can each take an end and lift her, like a stretcher."

The women could barely see through the haze in the room. Olivia coughed and hacked on the choking smoke. They moved Melissa from the bed and carefully placed her on the sheet. Each one grabbed an end and lifted her from the floor. Olivia put the axe under her arm and they shuffled towards the closet. Kayla pushed backwards through the hole in the wall.

"The smoke's heavy in here, too," Kayla wheezed. "We need to hurry the heck up."

Maneuvering the makeshift stretcher through the hole, Olivia hunched over and crawled through ... just as flames crashed through the door to Melissa's room. The girls lowered Melissa to the floor.

"How are we going to get Melissa down that

ladder?" Kayla's voice was high-pitched. She hacked on the smoke filling Olivia's bedroom. Their eyes stung.

Olivia flung open her closet door. She pulled scarves and belts from the hooks and tossed them on the floor. "Use the ropes to tie Melissa to my back. If there isn't enough, then use the scarves and belts."

Kayla stared at Olivia.

"There's no other way. I'm not leaving her. Help me get her up."

They pulled Melissa from the floor to standing position, holding tight to her arms. Olivia hunched over and shuffled her back up against the front of Melissa's body. She reached back for her arms and pulled her forward like she would give her a piggy back.

"Tie the ropes and belts around us," Olivia said. "Wind them tight."

"How is this going to work? You're not strong enough to do this." Kayla wound and tied and hooked the ropes and belts into place.

"We don't have a choice. What else can we do? We'll have to make it work. It's a good thing she's small. Open the window."

Kayla pushed the window up as far as it would go. She grabbed the axe and bashed at the window glass and the frame to make the space bigger. Kayla knocked Olivia's dresser over and slid it close to the window so that Olivia could step up onto it and get through the window more easily.

The bedroom door cracked, flames licked into the room and flashed up to the ceiling.

"Oh, hell," Kayla shouted.

Olivia stood frozen at the window, hunched over with Melissa on her back, her left hand reaching to hold Melissa's dangling arm and her other hand clutching the sill.

"Go," Kayla yelled.

Olivia looked at her. "I'm ... afraid."

"Get the heck out that window or I'll push you out," Kayla ordered Olivia.

Olivia swallowed hard. She leaned out of the window keeping her eyes on the escape ladder to avoid looking down. People had gathered on the lawn below and shouted for her to come out.

Olivia's heart hammered at her chest wall. *Please let this work.*

"Here we go, Mel," Olivia whispered. She reached for the metal rungs, trying to correctly balance Melissa's weight to keep from being pulled down backward.

She grabbed the first rung. Kayla leaned over the window sill and held onto Melissa by the ropes as Olivia swung her feet onto the rungs. *We're on! We're out!*

"Come on, Kayla! Get out of there!" Olivia wiggled her feet down from rung to rung, feeling with her toe for the next one. Her hands, wet with sweat, slipped on the metal ladder, but she held tight. Her muscles screamed from the load she carried on her back.

Down, down.

The last rung was positioned above the first floor windows, so Olivia would have to let go and drop from the bottom of the ladder. People rushed forward to break the fall.

Olivia held her breath. When she released her hold on the rung, she tried to hunch forward to keep from falling backwards on top of Melissa.

The two plummeted to the ground with a crash that knocked the wind out of Olivia's lungs. The side of her head cracked against the ground and pain shot up her leg and into her back.

She was flat on her side with Melissa still tied to her. *We're on the ground.*

Relief flooded Olivia's body. Through the black edges of her sparkling vision, she watched Kayla drop from the ladder and land beside her.

The screams of the fire truck tearing down the street filled the night air.

Olivia turned her head to Kayla. "*Now* they show up."

26

S irens. Feet pounding on the ground. Shouts.

Firefighters pulled hoses from the trucks as other emergency vehicles tore around the corner. A police officer ran to the women and knelt beside them.

"That damn, damn Eric Daniels did this." Kayla struggled to push herself to sitting position. "He set the damn fire. He kidnapped me." She waved her hand towards Melissa. "He injected her with something. He tried to kill us! He set the building on fire. He killed Christian and Gary and Jack." Sucking in a gasp, she gripped her right arm with her left hand. "I think I broke my arm." Kayla leaned back on the grass.

Cops and EMTs swarmed around them. They cut Melissa free from Olivia's back.

Melissa opened her eyes and moaned. "Liv?"

"I'm here, Mel. Everything's okay," Olivia said, still resting on her side.

"You need to find that monster," Kayla yelled. "Or I swear to God I will hunt him down myself."

Olivia couldn't help but grin at Kayla's ranting, but then her lips turned down. Rolling onto her back and looking up at the building, she watched the angry orange flames flashing against the night sky, the fire consuming her apartment. Olivia shifted her gaze to the metal rungs on the side of the building, grateful to whoever pounded each one of them into the wall. A strange sense of calm overcame her.

The women were placed on stretchers and moved away from the building to waiting ambulances. Police officers questioned Kayla and Olivia about what had happened as they were being transported to the vehicles. There would be more and more questions once they reached the hospital.

As they were loading her into the back of the ambulance, Olivia pondered the crazy and terrible things that people were capable of inflicting on each other and she realized that there wasn't a whole lot that anybody could do to stop it.

A tear escaped from her eye and rolled down the side of her face creating a little white trail in the soot that covered her skin.

∾

SEVERAL DAYS LATER, Olivia, Melissa, Kayla, and Ynes sat on the two twin beds in the cramped university dorm room eating Chinese food from takeout containers. After the fire destroyed their apartment, Olivia and Melissa were able to contract with the college for a double room to share for as long as they needed it. Insurance would cover the cost of their furniture, laptops, and some clothing.

"I'm really sorry I missed all the excitement," Ynes joked. "I still don't understand why you didn't wait to settle this until I got back from that conference in New York."

"Yeah." Olivia wiped some peanut sauce off of her chin and gave Ynes a pointed look remembering how she had taken out Adam Johnson in the parking lot behind the dance club. "You would have come in handy."

"You want some more rice, Kayla?" Melissa asked.

Kayla had a broken arm which was elevated in a sling. "Yes, please. It's amazing how people take the use of two hands for granted." Melissa scooped rice onto Kayla's plastic plate.

"How's your ankle feeling, Olivia?" Kayla asked before lifting a forkful of sesame chicken into her mouth.

"It's pretty good. The ace bandage helps. Even though it's just a sprain, I won't be jogging for a few weeks. I'm still limping on it." Her leg was propped up on a chair. She took a sip of iced tea and looked at Melissa. "I still can't believe we got down that ladder with you tied to my back." She grinned. "Next time I'll land on Melissa, not the other way around."

Melissa looked at Olivia and was about to say something, but her eyes misted over and she got choked up.

"Uh, oh," Kayla said. "Melissa's going to cry again."

Melissa cleared her throat and waved her hand in the air. "No, I'm not." Her voice was shaky. She locked eyes with Olivia and then with Kayla. "Thanks to both of you." A tear rolled down her cheek. "Thanks for not leaving me behind." She brushed at her cheek.

Kayla's eyes sparkled. "I told you she was going to cry."

"Leaving you was not an option," Olivia told Melissa. "You're the sister I never had. I prefer to keep you around a little while longer."

"So fill in some blanks for me before this gets too mushy," Ynes said. "How did this all happen?"

Kayla's face was serious. She gave a long sigh. "I still can't believe that bastard is the killer. And that I was with him so much and never suspected him." She moved her plate off her lap and placed it on the bed next to her. "Eric texted me that night. He said he found something that might be a break in the case. He met me at the café. He acted so excited about what he found. He said he used his computer systems knowledge to find it. He wanted me to come with him to his place as soon as I got off my shift. He had to show me what he discovered."

Kayla took in a long breath. "When we got to his building and we went into his room, I almost passed out. While I was staring at the pictures of me and Christian all over the walls, Eric pulled a knife on me. He put his arm around my neck, cut my arms. They were only superficial, but I was terrified. He made me text Olivia to meet me at the café. His original plan was to kill me and Olivia and Melissa at his apartment, but when Olivia texted that Melissa was sick, he changed his mind about the location. We took a cab to Melissa and Olivia's place. He threatened me to keep me quiet on the way there. He broke into their apartment. Melissa was asleep on the couch. He stuck her with a syringe. It was a sedative, one of those date rape drugs. It knocked her out. He made me help move her to the bedroom. I didn't know it, but he had small canisters of gasoline in his backpack. He had planned to knock us all out and then burn the building down." She brushed her hair away from her eyes.

"I was at the café waiting for Kayla," Olivia said. "I started to worry. She wasn't answering my text and the barista said she heard Eric say they were going to his apartment. It was a red flag to me because Kayla told me she had never been to his place, even though they had been friends for a couple of years."

Kayla picked up the story. "Eric wanted to knock us out one at a time. That's why he wanted Olivia to be at the café while he took care of Melissa." She looked at Olivia. "He was enjoying tracking you with his phone. He was amazed that you went to his building. He called you 'a worthy opponent.' I wanted to kill him. I tried to fight him when he was going to tie me up, but he said if I didn't cooperate that he would kill Melissa right then, right in front of me." A sob caught in Kayla's throat. Melissa put her arm around Kayla's shoulders.

"We assume he downloaded the tracking app onto my phone at the hospital when Kayla and I went to the restroom," Olivia said. She paused for a moment and then went on. "So when I was in his room, I saw the pictures, the computer tracking thing, the ski mask. He texted me, told me to go home and not to call the police or he would kill Kayla and Mel." The horror of the night nearly paralyzed her for a moment.

She turned to Ynes. "You know the rest."

Ynes gave Olivia's hand a squeeze.

"I should have known it was Eric." Kayla's energy had dissipated. She looked so small sitting on the bed next to Melissa. "I should have known he was the killer. The guys are dead because of me."

"You couldn't have known," Olivia said in a soft voice. "It's easy to look back and notice little things, but when we're living them, everything just seems normal. Just because he got fired, just because people didn't like him, those things don't point to a murderer. And he was always nice to you … caring, kind." Olivia blew out a breath. "It's not your fault, Kayla. Not any part of it."

Melissa said to Kayla, "Don't ever think that. It's Eric's fault. It's all because of Eric and his horrible obsession with you."

Olivia added, "If it wasn't you, Kayla, then it would have been someone or something else. He was sick." She sighed. "Obsessions. The all-consuming desire for something and the terrible things that can happen when that something is denied." She shook her head.

"I'm glad he's dead," Ynes said. "I'm glad the police killed him. There won't be any trial to drag you all through. It's over."

Eric was caught outside his apartment building. As the police were placing him under arrest, he grabbed one of the officer's weapons and shot the cop. Another officer took Eric out.

The four young women sat in silence not saying anything for a minute, and then Olivia turned to Ynes. "What about your friend from the gym? Eva. She must be relieved that Adam Johnson is in custody." Johnson had been charged with the murder of a young man from Dorchester which, to no one's surprise, was drug-related.

Ynes' eyes looked heavy with sadness. "Eva went

back to Venezuela. She's afraid of Johnson. Whether he's in prison, or not. I don't think she's coming back."

A knock sounded on the door. Ynes got up to answer it. The dorm supervisor stood there holding a glass vase filled with pink and lavender flowers. "These just came. They're for Olivia."

Ynes took them and placed them on the desk. She sat down next to Olivia and handed her the card that came with the flowers.

Olivia opened it.

"Well, who are they from?" Melissa asked, even though she had a pretty good idea who sent them. "Don't keep us in suspense."

Olivia looked up and groaned. "Guess who."

Melissa chuckled.

"What's funny?" Ynes asked. "Who sent them?"

"Jason," Melissa said. "The guy Liv met at the formal. She doesn't appreciate his persistence. Liv was sure that Jason was the one who downloaded the stalker app to her phone. She thought he went into her purse at the formal dance, took her phone out, and installed the tracking app."

Ynes raised an eyebrow and gave Olivia a sly smile. "So, are you going to give this guy a chance or what?"

"Oh, please." Olivia rolled her eyes. "Don't you start hassling me to date him, too."

Ynes reached for her purse. "Come on. How about

we walk, or hobble if you're Olivia, over to the pub. Drinks are on me. I think we should celebrate."

"What is there to celebrate?" Melissa asked looking around the cramped doom room.

Olivia swung her leg off the chair and stood up. She gave each of her friends a tender smile. "Being alive."

THANK YOU FOR READING!

To hear about new books and book sales, please sign
up for my mailing list at:
www.jawhitingbooks.com

Your email will never be sold, shared, or spammed.

If you enjoyed the book, please consider leaving a
review. A few words are all that's needed. It would be
very much appreciated.

ABOUT THE AUTHOR

J.A. Whiting lives with her family in New England. Whiting loves reading and writing mystery, suspense and thriller stories.

Visit me at:
www.jawhitingbooks.com
www.facebook.com/jawhitingauthor
www.amazon.com/author/jawhiting